Trail of the Heart

TRAIL OF THE HEART

SYLVIA GUILFORD

WestBow
PRESS
A DIVISION OF THOMAS NELSON

Copyright © 2012 by Sylvia Guilford.

All rights reserved. No part of this book may be used or reproduced by any means, graphic, electronic, or mechanical, including photocopying, recording, taping or by any information storage retrieval system without the written permission of the publisher except in the case of brief quotations embodied in critical articles and reviews.

ISBN: 978-1-4497-6359-6 (sc)
ISBN: 978-1-4497-6360-2 (e)
ISBN: 978-1-4497-6361-9 (hc)

Library of Congress Control Number: 2012914898

WestBow Press books may be ordered through booksellers or by contacting:

WestBow Press
A Division of Thomas Nelson
1663 Liberty Drive
Bloomington, IN 47403
www.westbowpress.com
1-(866) 928-1240

This book is a work of fiction. People, places, events, and situations are the product of the author's imagination. Any resemblance to actual persons, living or dead, or historical events, is purely coincidental.

Because of the dynamic nature of the Internet, any web addresses or links contained in this book may have changed since publication and may no longer be valid. The views expressed in this work are solely those of the author and do not necessarily reflect the views of the publisher, and the publisher hereby disclaims any responsibility for them.

Front cover photo: Sylvia Guilford
Back cover photo: Roger L. Shaw

Printed in the United States of America

WestBow Press rev. date: 09/20/12

Prologue

"WHAT ARE YOU CHILDREN DOING this far from camp? Your mother is worried. We are all supposed to stay near the wagons until Mr. McMasters, Mr. Gibbons, and Mr. Laurens get back from the settlement with the new scout."

"Jeremy was trying to catch a baby rabbit," explained his older sister, Meg, as the chubby-faced toddler nodded in agreement. "We didn't mean to come this far, Mrs. Brewster."

"Rabbit. Over there." Jeremy pointed.

"Yes, Jeremy, I see him. But we must not take him away from his family. I'm sure they must be nearby."

The little rabbit sat for a minute with its head slightly turned, watching them as it wiggled its tiny nose. Then with a little hop, the fluffy creature disappeared into the tall grass.

They stood watching for a moment to see if it would reappear.

"Oh, he's gone." Jeremy sighed with disappointment.

"Come! We need to go back to the wagons," Mrs. Brewster reminded them.

The three started in the direction of the wagons. The little rabbit had lured the children into a small grassy area surrounded almost entirely by thick underbrush dotted with trees. The lush prairie grass muffled the sound of their steps, and the tall growth surrounding them hid the wagons from view. Sallie Brewster felt relief at having found the children. The little ones could have easily lost their way. She would be glad to get them safely back to their family.

The previous afternoon, the man leading the wagons, McMasters, and two others had left for a settlement some distance from the trail. A message had been received that, due to an injury, the guide McMasters had been expecting would not be able to travel with them. McMasters was hoping to find a man to accompany them as a scout. He wanted a man with knowledge of the territory ahead who knew where water could be found and the best places to stop for the night with a group of wagons this size.

In addition to the injury, one of the men's saddle horses had lost a shoe and needed the attention of a smithy.

After McMasters gave strict instructions for people to remain close to camp during his absence, the three men departed for the settlement. He assured the travelers he would return the following afternoon.

The remainder of the afternoon was uneventful until three Indians rode into camp. Sallie remembered that the oldest one kept staring at her. They seemed harmless enough and just wanted to trade for some food. It wasn't long before they had departed. However, Harry Bailey had commented that morning that he was sure he had seen the Indians, or at least one of them, watching the wagons from a distance.

Sallie and the children had almost exited the grassy area. Suddenly, Sallie thought she heard something snap in the undergrowth nearby and had an uneasy feeling they were not alone. Pausing for a moment, she listened, but all was silent. *Maybe it was just an animal, a little rabbit*, she thought. But she felt a prickly sensation of fear and wished the children would hurry.

They continued in the direction of the opening out of the grassy area. Once they were out of this small, secluded meadow, Sallie and the children would be within sight of the large group of wagons parked near a sparkling stream.

What was that? Out of the corner of her left eye, Sallie thought she saw movement. Was it her imagination? With her heart pounding, she tried to think. *I have to get these little ones to safety! If someone or something is out there, they mustn't know I can hear them,* she thought. *We need time. Jeremy's little legs are so short, and he is too heavy to carry very far with any speed.*

"Meg, take your little brother's hand and go straight on back to your mother." Sallie calmly directed her. "You'll be able to see the wagons after you pass that last big tree. You hear?"

"Yes, ma'am." Meg nodded and, taking her brother's hand, turned to start back to the wagons. She glanced over her shoulder with a questioning look in her large hazel eyes.

"I'm coming right behind you. You hurry on back," Sallie urged, trying to keep the rising fear out of her voice.

Maybe it was nothing, Sallie thought. The children skipped ahead and rounded a clump of undergrowth that momentarily put them out of her sight as they headed in the direction of the wagon encampment. Just a few more steps and she too would be out of the secluded area and within sight of the wagons and the other families.

It was the last she saw of the children.

1

Three riders walked their horses along a dusty trail that gradually widened into the main street of a small but bustling town. One rider led an extra horse. People going about their business along the boardwalk or crossing the street barely noticed the strangers; westward-bound travelers often stopped for supplies.

Nothing about these men appeared out of the ordinary. The men reined their horses to a stop in front of a large board-sided barn near the edge of town. To one side of the barn stood a partial enclosure with a slanted roof. Inside this addition, a large, burly man with his back turned to the approaching trio was just lifting an object from the forge with a pair of tongs. He placed a piece of red-hot metal on his anvil and, picking up a large hammer with his free hand, began skillfully shaping the hot metal into a horseshoe.

The loud ringing of the hammer striking the hot metal startled one of the oncoming horses. All the horses approached the barn with ears forward, focused on the man with the hammer.

Pausing, the man turned the shoe over and, after studying it from several angles, dropped it into a nearby water-filled barrel. It made a hissing sound as it hit the cool water.

As the riders dismounted, the large man turned and with a nod acknowledged their presence. He laid down his tools and, stepping around a pile of metal on the ground, extended a large hand in greeting. His face was flushed from the heat of the fire.

"Hello," he greeted them in a surprisingly tenor voice. "You fellows must be new here. Don't recall making your acquaintance."

After a round of handshakes, Henry, the youngest of the three strangers, was the first to speak. With a gesture toward the sorrel he had been leading behind his mount, he explained, "Need your services. My mare threw her left hind shoe. Guess she's in need of a trim all around and new shoes."

Motioning for Henry to bring his horse inside, the blacksmith continued the conversation.

"Are you fellows with that group of settlers camped out by the Meadow Creek Crossing?"

"Yes, we are. Rode in to take care of this horse and pick up a few supplies. Also hoping to find a scout. The man who usually meets me at the Meadow Creek Crossing each year sent word he's laid up with a broken leg," McMasters explained his situation.

The smithy examined the shoeless hoof before commenting. "Truman Garrett's in town. He probably knows this country better than most men and can speak the Indian language as well."

The smithy then pulled the old shoe, trimmed and filed, and began working his way around the horse. Each foot was carefully examined. A few minutes went by before the conversation picked up again.

"Garrett's out back now looking over some stock of mine. Said he was interested in buying an extra saddle mount," the smithy said as he released a rear hoof and briefly straightened to study his handiwork.

As the leader of the wagons, McMasters felt uncomfortable leaving the people alone too long, because they looked to him for leadership. He really shouldn't have let both Grinder Gibbons and Henry Laurens accompany him to the settlement. However, Henry's horse had thrown a shoe, and there was no one traveling with the wagons skilled in blacksmithing. Grinder had come along since he knew of some men who might be in the area and willing to take on the job of scouting the trail for the settlers.

"We ought to go talk to him," Grinder said of Garrett.

McMasters hesitated, scratching his head. "Truman Garrett," he slowly repeated. "Seems I've heard that name before. Wasn't there a man some years ago by the same name with a reputation for being good with a gun?"

Grinder remembered the name too and nodded. "He never was known to go lookin' for trouble. Always kept on the right side of the law as I remember. Thought he was dead. Don't recall hearin' of him in years."

Henry's horse fidgeted as the blacksmith worked to fasten the new shoe. The horse settled down, and after the smithy tapped the last nail in place, he straightened and stepped away from the horse.

"Truman Garrett rides through here two, maybe three times a year. Quiet man, minds his own business. Nearly always rides alone. Years ago, I seem to remember an Indian with him, but that was a long time ago," the smithy recalled.

McMasters started out back in search of Garrett. He spotted a tall, lean, wiry, buckskin-clad figure leaning on a rail of the corral as he carefully looked over some half-wild mustangs circling within an enclosure. McMasters headed toward the man.

"Are you Garrett? Truman Garrett?"

The man slowly turned from the corral fence.

Not waiting for an answer to his question, the stocky, gray-haired wagon master continued striding toward the man at the corral.

"I could be," the man finally drawled.

"The blacksmith said I'd find you back here." Reaching out his hand, he briskly introduced himself. "I'm McMasters with the wagon train that's camped south of town."

With a nod of acknowledgment, Garrett reached to shake the hand offered him.

Getting right to the point, McMasters stated his business. "I hear you know the country west of here as well as any man. We'll pay you well to scout the trail and to get us to the mountains before cold weather sets in."

The stocky man spoke as one used to giving orders and as if he assumed the buckskin-clad man would be interested in the position offered, and was therefore surprised when the tall one didn't answer immediately in the affirmative.

Instead, Garrett scratched several days' growth of chin whiskers and commented, "Well, I was fixing to rest here in town a mite. Been eating my own cooking for months."

During the conversation, the other two men from the wagon train joined them. The older of the two, also dressed in buckskin, had a tangle of shoulder-length gray hair with a mustache of the same color that drooped down on either side of his mouth. He paused to spit a stream of tobacco to one side before he reached out his hand to Garrett. "Name's Grinder Gibbons. I believe we met some years back at Fort Bridger."

The tall one grunted and nodded as he shook the offered hand.

"Me and Henry here," Grinder explained, as he gestured toward the younger man beside him, "have been ridin' along with this group of settlers, keepin' 'em in fresh meat."

"Word came to us a couple of days ago there had been some Indian trouble up ahead. Don't want to take any chances."

"Seems to me I did hear of some difficulty west of here," the tall one agreed.

"Well, what do you say, Garrett?" McMasters pressed for an answer, impatient to make a decision, gather some needed supplies, and return to the wagons before dark.

"How much you willing to take for that bay?" Garrett directed his question to the blacksmith, who had appeared in the doorway of the stable as the men were speaking. After a brief haggle over the price, the deal was settled.

Turning back to McMasters, he asked, "How soon are you expecting to leave?"

Gesturing toward the nearby store, the wagon leader explained, "Need to pick up a few supplies and head back to the wagons soon as we can."

"I'll get my gear together and be ready to ride when you are."

2

A GENTLE BREEZE STROKED THE long prairie grass in undulating waves toward the horizon. A meadowlark voiced its melodious song as if to show appreciation of the surrounding beauty. Surely all was well in the warmth of the afternoon sun.

The four men reined to a halt at the top of a rise. Beyond them the hill sloped in a gradual descent to a wide valley intersected with a small stream that sparkled in the sunlight as it curved its way through open prairie, thickets, and cottonwoods. The wagon trail crossed the stream through a stand of gnarled old cottonwoods. A group of wagons were parked just to the east of the stream and woods. Livestock were grazing contently nearby with several older boys watching over them. People could be seen moving about among the wagons. From a distance, all appeared peaceful and organized.

However, as the men slowly descended the hill and approached the wagons, they became aware of a tense watchfulness on the part of the adults in the group. Men in the group either moved about with rifles tucked under their arms or standing at readiness nearby. The women were keeping their young ones close. As the horsemen drew near, a heavyset man with auburn beard and hair and wearing a clerical collar stepped forward to meet them. Close behind was a woman clutching two small children by the hand.

"Mr. McMasters, we fear Mrs. Brewster may have been taken by Indians," the man immediately informed, not waiting for the riders to dismount.

McMasters caught himself as he started to swear. Instead he asked, "What happened? How long has she been gone?" Then before anyone could answer, as if to release himself from any negligence, he reminded,

"Before I left for the settlement last evening, I told everyone to stay close to camp and not wander away from the wagons."

The man explained, "Our little boy and daughter wandered away from the wagons. We were all looking for them. Our daughter," he said, gesturing toward a little girl with long braids, "said she and her brother were chasing a rabbit in the trees over there at the edge of the blackberry thicket when Mrs. Brewster found them. Meg said Mrs. Brewster told the children to hurry straight back to the wagons. She was right behind them when they started back. But when the children had reached the clearing and were almost to the wagons, my daughter said she looked around and Mrs. Brewster was no longer behind them. Several of the men and I walked a ways into the trees calling her name, but there was no answer and we couldn't find any trace of her. That was about two hours ago. We don't know what to think. Early last evening, after you left for the settlements, three Indians rode into camp. They seemed friendly enough. Wanted to trade for some food and then rode out. At least we thought they left. Harry Bailey thought he saw an Indian as it was beginning to get light this morning. Said he was just sitting on his horse out there, watching us."

While the minister had been speaking, the four horsemen had dismounted and the other men and women of the wagon train had gathered around. McMasters removed his hat and stood running one hand through his silver hair. After seeming to study the ground for a minute, he turned to the new scout.

"Well, Garrett, I guess you can go take a look. See what you can find." Then, squinting in the direction of the sun, he added, "Expect there's still several hours of light. If the Indians got her, guess there isn't much can be done." Shaking his head as he started to lead his horse away, he muttered to himself, "Knew there was going to be trouble taking that widow woman along."

Truman Garrett turned to mount his horse, puzzled by that last remark, and felt a slight tug on the fringe at the bottom of his shirt. Looking down, he found two sets of big solemn eyes shyly peering up at him.

"Mister, please find her," the little girl pleaded with tears threatening to spill from her eyes as she clutched her little brother's hand. "It's our fault she's out there. Mrs. Brewster is our friend."

The little boy nodded agreement.

Their mother approached, and resting one hand on the little girl's shoulder and the other on her son's head, she spoke for the first time.

"I believe Sallie Brewster saved my children from someone or something. I pray you will find her. You *must* find her!"

"Yes, ma'am. I'll see what I can do." Garrett swung up on his grulla-colored mustang. With a nod and a respectful tug on the front of his hat for the mother, he turned to her husband and handed the minister the lead rope of his spare horse. Having done that, he rode out of camp in the direction he was told the missing lady had last been seen.

Upon reaching the little clump of trees and bushes near the stream, he dismounted and searched the ground with eyes long used to reading the story of tracks upon the earth. He swore under his breath, viewing the trampled state of the ground that had been hastily searched by the men from the wagons earlier. He gradually worked over the area until he found it: a single moccasin print. After further searching, he found were a pony had been ground-tied on the other side of the thicket. Near the spot where the pony had been standing, it looked like there had been a struggle. Some tender branches were broken, and there were some small boot prints. The pony's tracks led down into the steam bed, but not out on the other side. The Indian had ridden into the steam and headed away in its shallow water in an attempt to hide his tracks. Garrett mounted up and guided his horse along the steam as he carefully studied both banks for tracks departing the water.

After a while, the trail led out of the water, up the west bank of the steam, and through a sprinkling of trees and straggly undergrowth. Soon his horse was once again moving over gently rolling terrain covered with undulating waves of grass. He knew if he didn't catch up to them soon, he could lose their trail. There was only one set of tracks, so maybe he would be able to do something should he find them. If the Indian had met up with friends, that was another story. Just dealing with one of them would be risky enough. When he would come near the top of a rise, he would step down from his horse, remove his hat, and, leaving his horse behind, ease to the top of the hill and lie on his belly in the long grass to avoid being silhouetted on the horizon. After studying the prairie in all directions to the next faraway rise for any movement, he would mount up and let his horse lope off in the direction of the tracks, sometimes leaning forward off to one side of his horse's neck in an effort to spot any sign left by the Indian's pony.

Finally, after a number of repetitions of this, he was rewarded with a glimpse of some faraway movement—almost a dot on the landscape in the distance. Was it a horse, a buffalo, a deer? The more he studied it, the more he became convinced it moved in the manner of a horse, with at least one rider and a bundle or something crossways. The "dot" was headed down a long slope. There were a few huge, very old trees at the bottom. *There might be a stream there too*, he thought. He carefully planned his approach. If the Indian had meant to kill the woman, he would have done so back at the camp. But Garrett knew he had to be careful. There was no telling what would happen to her if the Indian felt threatened. It could be he had friends just over the next rise. Hadn't the people said three had ridden into camp the night before? Also, there could have been more than that waiting just out of sight.

Well, he would be careful. He would do what he could to rescue the woman, but he sure wasn't taking any unnecessary chances with his own skin. He judged, from the direction the Indian's pony was taking and the lay of the land, that he might be able to work his way around to cut them off and remain undetected for as long as possible if he didn't top over the ridge directly behind them but continued on a parallel track to them just below the top of the rise. Remounting, he urged his horse on in its seemingly effortless ground-covering lope. His horse was taller and rangier than the average mustang. While not being what some might consider beautiful, he was a powerfully built animal. The grulla-colored mustang with his great stamina and speed had outrun trouble more than once.

3

Throbbing head ... can't move ... on horseback ...

Without opening her eyes and with consciousness returning, Sallie took stock of her present situation. Lying across the back of a horse with her head dangling on one side and legs on the other, the pressure on her midsection was extremely uncomfortable. She willed herself to keep her body limp until she could more fully regain her senses. She tried to think back, to remember what had happened.

She had been on her way back to the wagons, anxiously peering around her after hearing that sound in the thicket. Suddenly, soundlessly from behind her—out of nowhere, it had seemed,—a hand had clamped over her mouth and an arm tightly surrounded her waist. She had tried to twist her head and had clawed with the nails of her free hand first at the hand over her mouth. She then tried to reach the face of her captor, but to no avail. Sallie tried kicking as she was lifted and carried through the thicket. She made contact several times, but the only reaction was an even tighter grip until she could hardly breathe. When her captor tried to throw her onto a waiting pony, she had struggled and managed to get both hands free. It was then she was hit with something. That was the last thing she remembered.

His head nodding slightly in rhythm to the horse's gait, the captor couldn't see her open one eye just a tiny slit to take in her situation. Buckskin clad leg ... moccasin ... the end of a long knife (apparently tucked somewhere above her range of vision in a waistband) ... horse's dun-colored shoulder ... long-stemmed prairie grass below, muffling the sound of the horse's steps ...

She let her eye fall back on the knife. *If I could somehow …* They seemed to be alone. She tried to think. One of the Indians the other night was riding a dun-colored horse when he rode into camp. It was the older one, with gray streaking his raven hair—the one who had kept staring at her. She didn't dare to twist to look at his face and thus let her captor know she was conscious. He hadn't killed her outright. Why? The children, had they made it back to the wagons and safety?

With one quick movement, Sallie pulled the knife from the Indian's belt and plunged it into his upper thigh. Hanging from the horse as she was, she couldn't reach higher with any force. At the same instant, she managed to push herself forward and to tumble headfirst from the horse's back. She had heard the Indian's groan as the knife went in and felt his fingers attempt to close around her arm or grab her clothing as she fell from the horse.

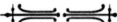

When next Garrett paused to peer over the rise, he was surprised at what he saw. Not only was he closer than he had anticipated, but the Indian had halted and the bundle, which turned out to be the woman, was giving him a really hard time. With the Indian distracted, trying to get her under control, this might be his time to move, he thought. He gave the horizon a quick scan for any unwanted company. Not seeing anything moving, he turned back to his horse and vaulted into the saddle, urging the animal over the crest of the hill and toward the struggle below.

When she hit the ground, Sallie rolled away from the horse. The Indian leaped from his horse and ran after her, the knife still protruding from his thigh, a stream of blood flowing from the wound and dripping down his dark-skinned leg. Even with the injury, he was very quick. Sallie sprang to her feet. Instead of trying to run, as he expected, she rushed forward and kicked him as hard as she could in his good leg. Twisting in an attempt to avoid his grasp, she lost her balance and fell. As the Indian bent over to grab her arm, Sallie rolled away from him, and as she did, she came into contact with a thick piece of broken limb from one of the nearby cottonwoods. Her hand quickly closed around it. Then, grasping it with both hands, she began swinging with all her might.

The first blow hit his head as he was bent over, reaching for her, and the next his shoulder as she managed to regain her footing. She struck him again and again. She kicked him hard again, this time in the injured leg, and he lost his balance. He tumbled onto the ground and rolled under the belly of his horse to the other side in an attempt to get away from her. She ran around the shying horse with the club raised for another strike. Blood was seeping from the place she had hit his head. The frightened horse swung around, striking out with a rear hoof, which probably saved the Indian from another blow as she dodged the animal. The Indian groaned and, getting up, attempted to straighten to an upright position with his horse between them. She saw a startled look come into his eyes as he seemed to focus on something behind her. She didn't dare take her eyes from him, but stood crouched ready to do more damage with the upraised club, which was actually somewhat shorter now, as a piece of it had broken away during one of the blows.

A chill went through her as a voice behind her said something in a language she did not understand. The Indian responded with something in his own tongue and made a kind of sweeping or pushing away motion with one of his hands. She heard a soft chuckle behind her. Finally daring to turn her head slightly, she beheld a buckskin-clad man mounted on a grulla-colored mustang with a Sharps rifle aimed almost casually in the Indian's direction. He said something to which the Indian grunted in reply. With a grimace, the Indian pulled the knife from his thigh. Then, limping, the Indian approached his horse and mounted somewhat clumsily. Turning toward the man on the grulla, the Indian said something else to which the other man responded. Then the Indian urged his pony forward and began to ride away.

As the Indian departed, Sallie turned to study the man in buckskin. Upon closer scrutiny of her rescuer, she wondered if she was truly rescued or in greater danger. This man certainly looked tough. He was lean and rangy like his mustang. He had the carriage and appearance of a man not to be taken lightly. There was several days' growth of beard on his face and a long shaggy iron-gray mustache drooping from his upper lip. Dark, piercing eyes, now focused on the departing Indian, peered out beneath heavy brows. Were he cleaned up, she decided, he might've been somewhat handsome, in a rugged sort of way. The man on the grulla mustang scanned the horizon, slowly lowered his rifle, and tucked it into a scabbard on the side of his saddle.

She took a deep breath and placed her hands on her hips. "What did he say?" Sallie demanded, hoping she sounded more confident than she felt.

He shifted his piercing gaze to her, taking in her somewhat disheveled appearance. In the struggle, some of her light brown hair with its streaks of gray had escaped the confines of the bun at the base of her neck. Her dress had a tear down one arm and another on the skirt. The dark-patterned material was smudged in places with dust and grime. As he silently studied her from head to foot, she tried to hide how uncomfortable he made her feel.

Again, she demanded, "What did he say?"

He looked her directly in the eyes.

"Said you were too much trouble, and I was welcome to you," he drawled in a deep baritone voice.

As he spoke he rested both hands on his saddle horn and leaned slightly forward over the neck of his horse. She thought she detected a somewhat amused light in his eyes, and that sparked her anger in spite of her situation.

"There surely was more to the conversation than that," she persisted.

"Ah, maybe a word or two …"

Sliding his left foot out of the stirrup, he offered his hand to pull her up with him on his horse.

Instead, she took a backward step. "I'm in no hurry to climb on a horse with another strange man. Who are you?"

Surprised by that response, he leaned back in his saddle and stroked a hand across the whiskers on his chin as he studied her.

"Lady, after what I just saw you do to that Indian, I'm thinking I'm the one taking the chance offering you a ride. Of course, if you'd rather walk back to your wagon …"

"Wagon? How do you know where I came from?"

"McMasters sent me to look for you, and a couple of little kids begged me to find you. They had the idea it was their fault you were out here."

"The children, they—they are all right?"

When he nodded, she continued.

"You must be the man Mr. McMasters went looking for at the settlements. We need someone to lead us to the mountains."

"Yes, ma'am, I reckon." He looked off to the western horizon. "Now, the sun is going to be setting over that ridge before long, and that Indian may have some friends waiting for him out there somewhere. He might just change his mind about having a white woman in his teepee. Do you mind if we get moving now?"

"Oh … of course."

This time, she took the hand offered her and managed to place her left foot in the stirrup that was so very high off the ground. She was surprised at how easily he pulled her up. The horse's sudden forward movement as she settled behind the man in the saddle forced her to grab the man's waist to keep from tumbling off the back of the horse, much to her embarrassment. Conversation was impossible. It took all of her concentration just to hang on and to keep her balance. She didn't dare wrap her legs too tightly around the horse due to where she was seated: tightening her grip near his tender flank might cause him to buck. Sallie was left with no alternative but to desperately cling to this stranger. After a time, her senses became aware that even though he was dust-covered and unshaven, he didn't smell of sweat. He had an air about him of buckskin and pine.

When at last the group of wagons came into sight, the sun had slipped under the horizon, leaving a few fluffy, orange-tinted clouds painted against a turquoise-hued western horizon. A soft afterglow lasted until they reached camp; darkness, however, had already claimed the eastern horizon.

Sallie pointed out her wagon to Garrett. He reined in his horse where indicated and allowed her to slide off.

"Thank you for coming to my rescue."

"Lady, you pretty well rescued yourself. I reckon I just gave you a ride back to your wagon."

Suddenly, Sallie felt a little body thump against her and a small pair of arms try to wrap around her skirt. She looked down into little Jeremy's big, smiling eyes. Meg was coming right behind him, followed by their mother and father.

"Thank God you are all right! We were so worried," their mother exclaimed as she hugged Sallie.

Some of the other families from nearby wagons were soon gathering around to see if she was indeed okay. They wanted to know what had happened. There was a flurry of questions. While Sallie answered them and assured them she was indeed unharmed, her rescuer slowly walked away, leading his horse through the crowd.

When Sallie thought to look around for him, it was growing dark, and her rescuer was nowhere in sight.

4

It was just starting to get light the next morning when Garrett rolled out of his blankets. He stretched and scratched at the whiskers under his chin. He decided he would dig into his saddlebags to find that piece of mirror and maybe shave this morning. That nice Higgins family had invited him back for coffee after sharing their meal with him last evening, and he didn't want to look too scruffy. He figured to check on his horses first and then go down to the stream to clean up.

After washing, he decided the Higgins family might appreciate a little fresh game. He felt especially obliged to contribute after their kindness the evening before. Seeing as how it appeared the families were just beginning to stir, he felt he had time to take a quick ride out to see if there was anything to be had. Catching up his horse, he set out.

Not having ridden far, he heard a shot. Looking off to his left, toward where he had heard the sound, he saw a boy running across an open area with a gun in one hand and what appeared to be a rabbit in the other. Out of the corner of his eye he caught movement. Upon turning his head, he realized the reason for the boy's hurry. A bear was charging and would surely overtake the lad before he could get to safety. Garrett reined his horse around in the direction of the boy and urged the animal to leap into a gallop. The boy was attempting to juggle both gun and rabbit as he climbed a tree when Garrett managed to get between boy and bear. Suddenly he realized it wasn't a boy. It couldn't be … He must still be half asleep. But, yes, it sure enough was that lady, Mrs. Brewster, dressed in britches and baggy shirt attempting to scramble up a tree.

"Jump on behind me!" he commanded as he pulled his mustang to a sliding halt next to the not-too-tall tree.

With a nervous glance over her shoulder at the approaching bear, she obeyed. Quickly handing him her rifle, she leaped from the tree to the rear of the horse. He touched his spurs to his horse just in time to escape. The grulla mustang, its ears laid back, lunged forward into a full gallop. Sallie hung on for dear life. Somehow she managed not to drop the rabbit in the excitement. After a distance, the bear gave up the chase, so they slowed their pace. Garrett slowed the grulla to a walk upon reaching the edge of the clearing, where the settlers where busily making ready for the day's travel. When it appeared he planned to cross directly through the middle of camp to her wagon on the far side, Sallie voiced her objection.

"Mister, please either stop here and let me dismount or walk your horse around the outside of the wagons to mine. I needn't be the topic of this morning's conversation dressed like this."

Smiling to himself, Garrett guided his horse around the outside of the wagon encampment as directed. Upon reaching her wagon, he halted his horse. After she slid down, he handed her the rifle.

"Again, I owe you my thanks."

"Lady, when you want fresh meat, I'll bring it to you. Don't you go out alone like that again."

He spoke sternly. With that said, he turned his horse and started to ride away. As he departed, he looked back over his shoulder, and with an amused gleam in his eye, taking her in from head to toe, commented, "Nice outfit."

"Darn you," she whispered to herself.

Hurriedly Sallie put up her rifle and took care of the rabbit. People were bringing in their stock to hitch up the wagons. A little knot of panic began to twist in her. She was late! What would McMasters say if she held up the wagons this morning because her teams weren't hitched and ready to go? Would that new man, Truman Garrett, tell McMasters about the incident this morning with the bear? Sallie quickly changed clothes, and, jumping down from the wagon, started to hurry in the direction of the livestock. With relief, she stopped in her tracks. There was Gil … dear Gil.

Oh God bless that boy! He was coming along the line of wagons toward her, leading one of her teams, and his little brother, Harry, was right behind him with her other team of mules. The gentle mules were trailing the boys with long ears alert. One of the mules let out a bray and was answered by another animal from one of the nearby teams.

"Good morning, boys. Thank you for bringing in the mules. I'm running a little late this morning."

"Yes, ma'am," they answered in unison."

Gil was a great hand and directed his brother in helping to harness the teams. While the boys took care of hitching the mules to the wagons, Sallie retrieved her horse, Joe, and tied him to the back of her first wagon. Soon they were ready. Harry hurried back to ride with his folks, and Sallie climbed onto the first wagon and picked up the lines. Gil proudly sat on the other wagon seat and held the reins of her second team of mules. At fourteen, Gil was taller than Sallie, and if his big hands and big feet were any sign, he would surely be a big man by the time he stopped growing. While the second team was not as impressive as the first, it was nonetheless a smart-looking foursome. Soon the command to start the wagons was given, and they were once again on their way westward.

Truman Garrett rode up to the wagons late in the afternoon. He was just dismounting from his horse after an afternoon of scouting the trail ahead of the wagon train. Grinder and Henry had ridden in and had already pulled their saddles. The elder of the two had just rolled a smoke and was lighting up. After taking a couple of draws to be sure he had it working, he informed Garrett of the supper plans.

"Hey, True, that preacher invited me and Henry to his wagon for supper tonight. He said to bring you along too. The preacher's wife and that widow lady share the cookin'. They's mighty good cooks."

"Sounds good to me," replied Garrett. "I've had enough of my own cooking for a spell."

Henry explained, "Nearly every night, if we time it right, somebody invites us to join them. This train is sure full of good cooks. Mrs. Carter—that's the wagon with the roan mules—Mrs. Schaefer, and Mrs. Brewster are the best. Now, you might want to stay away from the Willards at suppertime. Me and Grinder weren't rightly sure what that was Mrs. Willard served us up one time. Remember, Grinder? I was out in the woods about all night sick as a dog."

Grinder nodded his head, remembering.

"Thanks for the advice. I'll keep that in mind," replied Garrett as he lifted his saddle from the bay gelding.

"How'd that new bay of yours do? He looked a little rough when you rode out from the wagons at noon." Grinder was remembering the bucking fit the horse had started when Garrett had thrown a leg over the saddle.

"Ah, he settled down after a while. Just a little green, that's all."

Grinder nodded understandingly as he took another long draw on his smoke.

"Well, guess I'll go down to the water and wash off a little of this trail dust before we mosey over to the preacher's," decided Grinder.

"You're sprucin' up for that widow lady," Henry teased with a smile.

"Ah, no, I ain't." However, the accused looked a bit embarrassed as he turned to head down to the stream.

"Reckon I could do with a little cleaning myself," decided Garrett.

Henry decided he might as well tag along.

The sun was descending as a bright red ball in a cloudless sky as the three men made their way toward the preacher's wagon. Greetings were exchanged in passing with some of the other families.

The preacher greeted the men with a hearty hello and handshake. A large kettle was braced over the cook fire. The women were taking turns stirring the steaming stew and fussing over the children. The three quests seated themselves on a long board the preacher had laid across the top of two stumps of about the same height, making a kind of bench. The four men were soon involved in a discussion of the day's findings as the preacher pumped them with questions about the trail ahead and the game seen in the area. Earlier in the afternoon, Grinder and Henry had distributed meat from a couple of deer they had killed for the wagon train. Garrett had seen no sign of any Indian ponies. The trail seemed to be in pretty good condition for this time of the year. In a few low-lying areas, the trail ahead was still soft from a heavy rain the week before and rather deeply rutted from earlier wagon trains passing through—but nothing bad enough to cause them worry. Thus, the men chatted until the food was ready to dish up and the minister offered the blessing.

It was a delicious meal. Garrett had to admit that Grinder and Henry were right when they had said these ladies put out a good spread. It amazed him how some women seemed to be able to adapt to the harsh and uncomfortable conditions of the trail, while others complained and couldn't seem to cope. He kept noticing the widow he had rescued. She was a handsome woman. Obviously, some of the other older men thought that too, for he noticed several looking her way as they passed by the wagons.

The light was fading, and the women had washed and cleared away most of the utensils. Little Jeremy was yawning and rubbing his eyes with his chubby hands. He looked like he could almost nod off right were he sat playing with some wooden figures his father had carved for him. His mother decided to get the children ready for bed. Mrs. Brewster reached to pick up a heavy kettle and started toward her wagon.

"Let me carry that for you," offered Garrett.

"Oh, thank you."

"That certainly was a good meal. That rabbit meat in that stew was mighty tasty too," he said, glancing sideways to be sure she got his drift.

"I'm glad you enjoyed it, Mr. Garrett."

He set the kettle into the back of the wagon where she directed and turned toward her.

"Ma'am, I'm not attempting to tell you what to do, but don't be wandering away from the wagons in the morning. Might be more than a nest of bears out there."

"I shouldn't need to. Henry and Grinder brought in enough venison for all of us."

"Night, ma'am."

"Good night, Mr. Garrett, and thank you."

With a tug to the front of his hat, he turned and walked away.

Sallie's gaze followed him until he disappeared into the darkness beyond the glow of the fire's light. There was something about that man that drew her interest. He seemed different from anyone she had ever met. Oh well. She was too tired to dwell on it. She took a quick look to be sure she'd picked everything up and turned in. The ordeal the day before with the Indian had left her bruised and sore.

5

THE CAMP WAS BUSTLING WITH activity shortly after sunrise the next morning when the difficulty became apparent. Jarrod Larson, a lean, red-faced man with little patience, was leading a young sorrel gelding toward his wagon.

A glint of light off metal or a bit of cloth flapping may have caught the animal's eye. It was hard to tell for what reason the sorrel suddenly shied and balked. The man was already in a bad mood and cussed as he jerked on the lead rope. The sorrel, its head up, rolled his eyes and shied again. This time the horse stepped on Larson's foot as he sidestepped. Still cursing, his face getting even redder than it normally was, Larson spied a whip leaning against a neighboring wagon within his reach. His hand shot out and snatched it up. He popped the horse on the shoulder.

This only served to make a bad situation worse. The already frightened horse, feeling the sting of the whip, lunged backward. The angry man stumbled and nearly lost his balance as he grasped the lead rope in one hand and the whip in the other. Larson began to lash out again and again with the whip as the horse reared and plunged, jerking the cursing red-faced man along with him. A gash had opened on the horse's face just below his eye. The commotion was beginning to draw attention from some of the other people, but no one attempted to intervene.

Sallie was leading her mules to her wagon when she became aware of a disturbance on down the line. Quickly tying the mules to the side of the wagon, she hurried to see what was going on. As she approached and realized what was happening, she was horrified that no one was lifting a hand to stop the beating.

She turned to the nearest man and asked, "Why doesn't anyone stop that man?"

The answer she was given was this: "It's his horse."

Sallie pushed her way between two of the men. The animal was now bleeding from the shoulder and squealing with each blow as it continued to plunge and jerk the cursing man along with him. As the man's arm swung backward to levy another blow at the gelding, he felt the whip catch on something and it would not come forward. He jerked again and again, but it held fast. Turning, he saw the reason. The widow lady had managed in a lightning grab to catch hold of the narrow strip of whip leather. Now, gripping it in both hands and bracing both feet, she was hanging on tightly. He tried again to jerk it away from her and succeeded in nearly pulling her off her feet, but she hung on.

"Damn it, woman, it's my horse, and I'll teach him a lesson if I've a mind to. Let go!" He bellowed.

With his attention directed momentarily to her, he was somewhat off balance when the horse reared again. In trying to hang on to the lead rope, he lost his hold on the whip handle. Sallie Brewster was able to yank it away from him.

"Someone ought to use this on you! You—you horrible man!"

With that, she turned, and, nearly running into a man standing behind her, she shoved the whip handle into his surprised hands. The man nearly missed it, and the handle struck him hard in the midsection, resulting in him expressing a surprised-sounding "wump."

"Don't you dare let him have this back!"

Her intervention seemed to have stirred the bystanders out of their almost trance-like state. Two men then intervened. One man stepped between Larson and his horse and another started trying to calm Larson down.

Shaking with anger herself at the senseless beating of the horse, Sallie returned to her wagon. It wasn't until she reached her mules and was untying their leads in preparation to hitch them to the wagon that she felt her hands stinging and discovered the narrow whip leather had sliced into her tender flesh as Jarrod Larson had attempted to jerk it away from her. There were drops of blood oozing from cuts on the palms of both hands. It was going to be painful holding onto the reins today. It hurt just trying to grasp the harness and buckle the mules in place. Well, she had done what she had to do, so she'd just have to get on with the day. With determination, Sallie took hold of the harness straps. She was startled as an arm reached over her shoulder and a man's hand took hold of the leather strap she was attempting to buckle. She hadn't been aware of anyone's approach.

"I'll do that for you. Get something on those hands."

"I'm all right."

She started to protest, but Truman Garrett had already gently taken the harness leathers from her and was fastening one of the mules in place. Walking around to the side of her wagon, she took a bottle out and began dabbing a liquid over the broken skin.

"From the look of those hands, you're going to be mighty uncomfortable for rescuing that horse." His tone puzzled her.

"You don't think I should have done anything?" she asked incredulously.

"It's Larson's horse."

"So? You mean that you wouldn't have done anything?"

"None of my business, lady."

"I don't believe that."

He just gave her a look over his shoulder as he fastened the last buckle. He made sure the reins were untangled and wrapped them loosely around the brake handle before turning to her.

"What did you put on those cuts?"

She held up the bottle to show him.

"If your hands are giving you trouble tonight, I know something that might help. Don't want to let a cut get to festering out here."

"What do you use?"

"Oh, it's an old Indian recipe. Seems to work."

He offered her help in climbing onto the wagon seat. It was time to get started.

Their eyes met. She realized she wanted to know more about this man who once again had come to her aid. There were more questions she wanted to ask, but she simply said, "Thank you for helping me hitch the mules."

He nodded, and, touching the front of his hat, he turned to his horse that had been waiting patiently nearby. He stepped into the stirrup and gracefully mounted. The horse, feeling fresh and rested, moved out with a shake of his head and a spring in his step.

Sallie's gaze followed horse and rider until she was distracted by the "Wagons roll!" command called out by the wagon master at the head of the line. Wagons began to move. Her mules didn't even wait for her urging; when the wagon in front of them began to roll, they started forward. After the many days of travel, they knew what to do. She had a good team. Fletcher and Foster were closest to the wagon. Both were big and powerful and dark bay in color. The lead mules, Jasper and Rocky, were lighter in color. Jasper had more of a mahogany hue to his coat, while Rocky's coat was a dusty brown. The jingling of the harness and creaking of the wheels were sounds of the trail that would be forever etched in her memory. Tied to the back of the wagon was her beloved saddle horse, Joe. The black/bay horse obediently followed along behind with head held high and ears pricked forward, taking in the sights and sounds of the prairie.

Once again, Gil was aboard Sallie's second wagon. While the second team was not as impressive as the first, it was nonetheless a smart-looking foursome. Close to the wagon were well-matched, muscular bays, Tug and Mac. In front of them pulled a brown mule named Dan and a roan mule named Spinner. The second wagon carried mostly feed for the mules and some spare parts for the wagons. She planned to eventually sell that rig.

The sun was directly overhead when Sallie came out of her daydream about mountains and green valleys and seeing her son, Jim, and his wife again. Her son and his wife had traveled westward a couple of years ago, saying they would send for her when they became established. Last fall, the long-awaited letter had arrived with the invitation that, if she was still of a mind to come westward, to come on out. A long list of things she would need to make the journey and to set up housekeeping in the new land was included with the letter. She would miss friends and family in eastern Iowa, but her son, his wife, and her grandchildren were out West. That was where her heart was, so she decided to follow her heart and had set about preparing for the journey. She knew some people thought she was crazy, and maybe she was. At her age, she was giving up what security she had to venture into the unknown.

Sallie wondered when she had ever felt so very alone as she scanned the horizon in every direction. The rolling prairie certainly had a way of making one feel isolated. Except for the people with the wagon train, there was absolutely no one out there. She knew because her wagon had reached the crest of a long slope. For miles ahead and behind, there was nothing to behold but rolling, grass-covered hills. However, the old wagon trail stretching ever westward beneath her proved to her that others had passed this way. The ever-present breeze whispered through the grass and played with the canvas cover over the wagon, causing it to ripple and flap. After adjusting her bonnet to better keep the sun off her face, Sallie pressed a hand to the small of her aching back and tried to change to a more comfortable position on the wagon seat. She had laid an old quilt over the wooden boards of the seat, but after a while, even that was of little comfort. Sallie wished she could get down and walk a while, but of course that was impossible since she was traveling alone.

In the beginning, she had made arrangements with a young man to accompany her and to help with the harnessing and the driving. She had two wagons and two teams of mules. The first wagon contained clothing, bedding, cooking utensils, a camp stove, food and a few treasures from her former home. The second wagon contained mostly feed for the livestock, spare parts for the wagons, extra canvas, tools, a tent, etc. She drove one wagon and Billy drove the second one.

However, one morning he was gone without a word. He, apparently, had been impressed with tales of gold strikes and easy riches to be had that were told by several men who had visited the travelers one evening. Anyway, the next morning their nearby camp was empty, and Billy was gone. Sallie guessed he felt the wagon train would be too slow for him. He could have at least waited to talk to her instead of sneaking off during the night.

When McMasters had discovered Billy had left her, he had threatened to have her pull her wagons out and leave her at the next settlement. The wagon train's leader didn't feel a woman alone could keep up with the rest of the train, and he said he sure wasn't going to have anyone or anything slowing him down. She had had to do some quick thinking and some mighty persuasive talking to convince him that she could handle caring for the teams and wagons alone. The preacher, seeing her predicament, had offered help if she ever needed it, for which she was extremely grateful, and fourteen-year-old Gilbert Grayson's dad had offered to let Gil replace Billy at driving one of the teams.

Sometimes, though, she felt McMasters was just watching for her to fall behind or break down. For this reason, she always made sure her wagons were the first hitched and ready to go every morning. Special attention was paid to checking the harness and the wagons to catch needed repairs before a breakdown. Of course, she took good care of her livestock. It showed too. Their coats were glossy, and they had a spring in their step. She had chosen well in the beginning, having a discerning eye for good animals, and she knew how to care for them and to keep them in good shape.

Sallie was brought back to the present with a jolt as a wheel of the wagon lurched over an especially large stone in the road. She should have been paying better attention and tried to steer the mules around it instead of drifting off with her thoughts. It was a wonder the wheel wasn't damaged. She leaned over the side to make sure everything looked okay.

McMasters announced they would be passing through a settlement with the chance of replenishing their supplies the next day. By now much of the food and animal supplies carried in Sallie's second wagon had been consumed. The teams had become accustomed to eating the prairie grass and were maintaining the strength and muscle needed to travel all day. Sallie believed in providing the hard-working animals with grain twice a day. However she decided she could sell the smaller wagon and the second team now.

By midmorning of the following day the wagons were rolling along the main street of a small town. While not a large community, it obviously was a prosperous and expanding one. Many of the buildings were new, with construction advancing at the edge of town. People hurried along the boardwalks in front of the stores with little more than a curious glance at the wagons.

Spotting a sign with the words "Arnold's General Store," Sallie pulled her wagon out of the line and over close to the boardwalk in front of the store. She leaned to her right as far as she could, and, looking behind to Gil on the wagon following, pointed to the sign. A middle aged man who had been standing in the doorway watching the wagons pass by stepped forward as the two wagons pulled to a halt.

"Good morning. I'm Arnold Webb. May I be of help?" he said.

"Good morning," Sallie responded. "Yes, I am in need of a few supplies."

She climbed down from the wagon, and, leaving Gil with the two wagons, followed Arnold Webb into the store. Some of the other people from the wagon train were already crowding into the store and being helped by a young man and an older woman.

"I need a bag of flour and a little salt."

As he pulled the requested items from a shelf and placed them on the counter, Sallie pointed to a jar of candies on the counter and said. "I'd like a couple of those stick candies too." Arnold nodded

As she was handing him the money for the items purchased, Sallie asked, "Do you happen to know of anyone needing a team and wagon? I am considering selling my second team."

Arnold paused. "Well, I've been thinking I could use another one myself for deliveries. I'll carry this out to the wagon for you and take a look at your team."

After a brief discussion, they were able to agree on a price. Sallie was pleased with her efforts. There were some items taking up space in the first wagon that she also decided to sell in order to make room for the few items she would need to transfer to the larger wagon from the one being sold. Arnold also offered to buy those few items she wished to sell. Sallie was careful not to add stress to the animals she was planning to keep.

Very carefully, Gil helped her repack everything so that the load was balanced before they pulled away from the store. Gil, relieved from his duties of driving her second wagon, offered to drive her primary team whenever she wanted a break, and Sallie agreed. In fact, she allowed him to drive as they left the little town. As they sat on the wagon seat together, she shared the candy purchased in the store. Feeling that another milestone in her westward journey had been successfully crossed with the sale of the second wagon, Sallie was soon lost in thought as she planned how she could best use the money from the second team and wagon.

Grateful for the many friendships she had made on the trip, Sallie tried not to be bothered by petty comments from a few of the women. There were some who insinuated there was something improper about a woman traveling alone. Once, Sallie had overheard a comment made by Harriet Pierce to some of her cronies that they had better all keep an eye on their men with "that widow woman flouncing around." Harriet always seemed to have her long nose in the air or her head turned away when Sallie passed by. Sallie usually responded to the snub by making sure she called a loud cheery hello to Harriet, to which she usually received a begrudged grumble or nod.

6

Truman reined his mustang to a halt at the crest of an especially high rise of ground. He was some distance ahead of the wagons and could see for miles. At first glance, there was no sign of any living thing in the rolling expanse ahead. Upon closer inspection, he saw a hawk circling in the sky to his right. To his left, far away beyond a few lower hills, he saw some dark objects that at first appeared stationary. After a few moments of study, it became apparent that there was a slow movement—probably a buffalo herd grazing. It appeared to be a small herd that would be crossing the trail and gone long before the wagons came along. On the far horizon, faintly etched against the sky was a bit of ragged green outline. That should be the cottonwoods along the creek where they would camp this evening.

His thoughts drifted back to Mrs. Brewster's confrontation with the man and his horse. She seemed surprised that he hadn't favored stepping into the situation. Maybe there was a time when he would have done something. Trying to help had gotten him into more than one scrape in the past.

Trouble had seemed to camp on his doorstep when he was a young man. Life had dealt him many a hard blow. Eventually, he had become hardened and had convinced himself it was best for him not to get too close to anybody. He had become somewhat of a loner.

What was it about Sallie Brewster that stirred him to remembering—remembering people and places long buried in his heart and mind? Did she in some way remind him of Carrie? She didn't really look anything like her, but there was that same gentle determination about her. Carrie was always helping someone. It seemed in her nature to always be reaching out to help a neighbor or stranger in need. What was it she had often said? "If a stranger needs help, then they are our neighbor." Well, trying to help a sick neighbor had caused her death and that of their little girl. First little three-year-old Amy came down with the fever, then Carrie. He remembered the ache in his heart as he stood by their graves on that cold, bleak February afternoon so many years ago.

After losing his wife and daughter, he had lost interest in the home and the land they had nurtured into a promising homestead. When he first drifted away, he had told himself it was just for a little while; he'd go back in a summer or two. It was just too hard to walk through that empty cabin, to see Amy's rag doll on her empty bed and Carrie's favorite yellow daffodils blooming in the yard. That was over twenty years ago.

He had always been a good marksman with rifle or pistol. The frontier had need of men with his talents. Gradually, he drifted further west. He was a quiet man, one who avoided trouble if possible. However, he was a mighty tough contender if circumstance left him no choice but to fight, be it with fist or gun. After he had drawn his gun on a bully who had left him no other choice, word began to travel about this Garrett who was mighty fast on the draw. He hadn't wanted to kill the man, but he'd been left with no choice. The local constable knew it wasn't Truman's fault, but the bully had kin who wanted revenge. The lawman wanted no trouble in his district and told Truman it would be best if he moved along. There would be further instances when he would need to be quick with his gun. Soon this ability made his name one to be respected where his gun was concerned.

Through it all he had managed to keep his name clean—until Dumas. He had ridden into the town one fall day looking for work. A man named Harley said he needed a hand to help him run some stock up in the hills. Harley was a recent addition to the area himself. It turned out he was not an honest man. However, he was so good at deceit that Garrett was in too deep before he realized something was not right with Harley's operation.

When a stranger from Harley's past rode into town, Garrett was told the stranger was an outlaw and had a grudge to settle with Harley. Harley begged Garrett to help him. Too late Garrett discovered that he had been taken in by Harley. The truth had been turned upside down. The stranger turned out to be the law. Truman Garrett was left holding the bag and spent some time behind bars. It certainly looked like he was in cahoots with Harley, and it took quite some time to clear his name. By the time Garrett was finally released, Harley had disappeared.

After that experience, Truman pushed further west. The knowledge of how he had been taken in by Harley ate at Truman's conscience. He disappeared into the hills.

Later he worked as a scout for an army post for a while. That was where he met Gray Fox, another scout for the army post. They struck up a friendship that lasted many years. Gray Fox invited Truman Garrett to come with him and live with his people after their days as scouts for the post were over. Truman took him up on his offer and lived with the Indians for many years. He learned to speak their language and to understand their ways.

At last, the lead wagons were approaching the evening's resting spot. Sallie's wagon was near the end of the line. She was so tired of sitting. It was such a relief to finally rein the team to a halt and step unsteadily to the ground. She began unhitching the team, her hands just slightly stiff and sore from yesterday's confrontation, but it wasn't so bad. Gil helped her get them out of the harnesses. Afterward, Sallie assured him that she could manage watering the team. Again expressing how grateful she was for his assistance, she sent him back to his folks.

The livestock needed to be taken care of before all else. Leading the four mules down the slight incline beneath the cottonwoods to water was easier said than done. With lead ropes grasped in both hands, Jasper and Rocky's leads were in her left hand, and Fletcher and Foster's were in her right. Jasper was in a hurry, as usual, pulling on his lead rope slightly ahead of her; Rocky was trying to keep in step with Jasper, as was his habit. The big guys, Fletcher and Foster, were just poking along behind. The result was that Sallie felt like she was being pulled in two directions.

Then Fletcher butted her in the back with his head when she paused in her stride, attempting to maneuver over some large tree roots jutting up out of the earth near the water's edge. Sallie let out a surprised shriek as she tried to regain her balance, and managed to do so after a couple of stumbling steps that set her boots into the mud just inches from the water. Her arms stretched wide, the taut leads on either side of her brought her up short and kept her from tumbling headfirst into the stream. Fletcher snorted and shook is head as he lowered his nose to the water for a drink. Rocky was on Sallie's immediate left and extended his nose to the water.

A soft chuckle sounded behind her. Standing in the middle of her mules with Jasper and Rocky drinking on her left and Fletcher and Foster on her right, Sallie turned her head to see who it was. Truman Garrett was leading his ride of the day down to water.

"Thought for a minute there you were thinking of taking a little swim," he teased with a sideways glance. Truman wasn't able to completely conceal the smile looming at the corners of his mouth.

Sallie, a bit aggravated and breathless from the near-plunge into the water, just gave him a look. She was sure blood had rushed to her face.

"The water's a bit cleaner up stream there," he said with a gesture in that direction. He just couldn't let it go.

"Oh, hush!"

The grin succeeded then.

"How're the hands?" he inquired, sensing it might be wise to change the subject.

"Okay," she assured him.

However, he let go of his horse's reins and stepped around the mules to see for himself. "Let me see."

He reached out and took the now slack leads from her left hand to his, and with his other hand, he examined her palm until he was satisfied all indeed looked okay. This he repeated on the other hand. She looked up and for a moment their eyes met. Then, with a grunt, he handed back the leads and strode back to his mount.

"You're welcome to come to supper with us, Mr. Garrett."

"Thank you, ma'am." With that, he touched the brim of his hat and, taking up his reins, led his mount up the incline through an opening in the cottonwoods toward the wagons.

After getting the team settled and watering her saddle horse, Joe, Sallie rushed to get started with the evening meal. The other women, with husbands to care for their livestock, already had preparations underway by the time she stepped to the rear of her wagon and, after loosening the rope that held the canvas in place, began pulling out the things she would need.

The minister's wife, Marta, was adding a few buffalo chips to the fire she had started as Sallie carried her heavy iron kettle over to join in the meal preparation. Even with the cottonwoods nearby, there wasn't much wood available for the fire. Occupants of previous trains had picked the campsite clean of that kind of fuel. That was okay, though, because everyone had become accustomed to gathering buffalo chips for fuel. Oh, some of the women still fussed about it. Hattie Lou Mercer flatly refused to touch the things, and made her husband pick them up and start the fire every night. Usually a kind of sling was kept under the wagon bed where chips or the occasional stick could be gathered along the way and kept dry for the cook fire. One never knew what might or might not be available at the next night's campsite. There might be neither wood nor buffalo chips, so it was a good idea to keep something under the wagon, just in case.

"Have you seen any of those scouts?" Marta asked as Sallie approached. "I wanted to be sure to invite them to eat with us again. Those men have been so helpful with providing meat to the train. I want them to realize how much we appreciate their help. I think some of the people are put off by their rough appearance and manner, but they are really goodhearted men."

"I haven't seen Mr. Gibbons or Mr. Laurens this afternoon, but Mr. Garrett brought his horse down to drink while I was watering the mules, so I reminded him he was welcome to eat with us," responded Sallie.

"You know, I think that man is taken with you," commented Marta as she began to mix some cornmeal for biscuits.

"Oh, Marta, surely not!" exclaimed Sallie, shocked that the younger woman had made that observation. "Whatever would make you say that?"

"I've noticed the way he watches you when you aren't looking. He'll be talking to my husband or one of the other men, but his eyes will be following you."

"Oh, he has probably just been out in the hills alone so long he'd watch any woman. I figure I'm too old to be concerned."

"You've heard the caution that there aren't enough women to go around out here."

The direction of the conversation rapidly changed as Meg slipped behind her mother and with a somewhat muffled squeal attempted to hide behind her skirts. Little brother wasn't far behind with something clutched in his grubby little hands. He stumbled to a halt with his newfound "treasure."

"Jeremy, what do you have?" asked his mother.

"It's just a little toad. See?" He held it out for all to see.

"Jeremy, put that creature back where you found it. You'll get warts!" His mother exclaimed.

"Warts?" he asked with a puzzled expression, wondering what that was. It must be something really terrible from his mother's tone—and just when he thought he'd finally found a pet!

"Those are bumps on your skin just like those on that toad's back," his mother explained. "Go right now! Put it back!"

"Oh." He hung his head and turned to take the now wiggling creature back.

"Wash your hands after you turn it loose. You and Meg can each have some carrot sticks when you get back. That'll hold you over until suppertime."

That promise helped only a little as he reluctantly shuffled off with the toad.

Meg came out from behind her mother's skirt after her brother had departed with the toad. Her job was to keep an eye on her little brother. However, as long as he held that toad, she followed at a safe distance.

Jeremy reluctantly set the toad down near the tree where he had found it and squatted down, watching it as it just sat there motionless, watching him back. He heard someone coming and looked up to see Mr. Garrett rolling his sleeves up as he made his way back down to the stream to wash up for supper, having taken care of his horses. The tall man paused, seeing Jeremy squatting with his hands on his knees, peering at something on the ground.

"What you got there, boy?"

"A toad. But I can't keep him," Jeremy said with a downcast sigh. Then he added with authority, "Toads give you warts."

Truman smiled. "Really?"

"Yes, sir. Mother says I need to wash my hands after I put it back."

"Well, I was just headed to the water myself. Need to clean some of this trail dust off before supper. We could walk down there together."

Jeremy nodded and walked along beside the tall, buckskin-clad man.

"Hey, girl." Truman acknowledged Jeremy's big sister, who had been keeping an eye on her brother, a safe distance from any possible contact with the toad. She smiled and trailed along behind them.

Jeremy walked along quietly for a few steps. He felt comfortable with this man and liked him. Mr. Garrett really seemed to listen when he talked, so the little boy searched his mind for something to say in the way of conversation.

"I heard my mother say to Mrs. Brewster that she thinks you are taken with her."

Well, he certainly got Mr. Garrett's attention with that one.

"Jeremy!" A horrified Meg attempted to hush her brother.

Undaunted, Jeremy continued, "But Mrs. Brewster said you'd probably just been out in the hills too long."

"Jeremy, hush! You talk too much," admonished his sister.

Mr. Garrett, struggling to suppress a laugh, agreed, "Well, I guess I have been out in the hills a mighty long time."

Later that evening, after the meal, when he had again offered to carry the heavy kettle back to Mrs. Brewster's wagon, he couldn't resist commenting.

"You're a mighty handsome woman, Mrs. Brewster. I'm of a mind that a woman ought to be told that kind of thing," He couldn't help saying, a twinkle in his eye. "Of course, I have been out in the hills a long time."

His unexpected comment brought Sallie up short. She tried to think of a comeback, but for once she was too struck to respond. All she was finally able to blurt out was a simple "Oh … um … thank you, Mr. Garrett." She continued strolling toward her wagon.

Truman remembered the spot where the kettle was kept, and made sure it was secure. He turned toward Sallie, paused for a moment, looking into her eyes, and seemed about to say something. The light of the rising moon shone on her face.

Sallie stood for an awkward moment looking up at Truman. She couldn't really read his expression, as his face was in shadow. The rising moon was behind him.

"You were kind to carry the kettle back to the wagon for me. Thank you."

"You're welcome, ma'am," he responded.

Truman touched the front of his hat and turned to leave. After taking a few steps, he stopped and turned partly around.

"Mrs. Brewster, if you have a slicker in your wagon, you'd best keep it where you can get to it easy. I figure with that ring around the moon tonight, we might be in for a little rain tomorrow."

"I'll keep that in mind."

He wasn't in a hurry to leave. It was comfortable being with her. He just couldn't think of anything else to say.

For a moment, Truman stood silently studying the sky.

Stars shone like a vast canopy of twinkling jewels set against a backdrop of black velvet. Here and there to the west, patches of sky were devoid of stars where soft dark clouds were drifting like shadows in the night.

"The sky somehow seems so much bigger and closer out here," observed Sallie. "Back home we always had so many trees around that we never really saw this much of the sky at one time. It makes me feel small and insignificant."

Truman nodded his understanding.

"Mrs. Brewster, if you don't mind my asking, what makes a woman like you leave your home and head out across this prairie alone like you've done?"

"Please call me Sallie. And I don't mind your asking." She paused, reflecting on the past that somehow now seemed so long ago and far away.

Sallie reached up behind the wagon seat and pulled down her shawl and wrapped it around her shoulders to keep back the chill of the evening air.

She began, "My husband didn't come back from the war. I waited, hoping maybe the notice I had received was wrong. My neighbor had been told her husband had been killed, but there was some kind of a mix-up, because he came back when it was all over. I kept thinking maybe …"

"Our son, Jim, and his wife decided to move west. They wanted me to go with them, but I didn't feel I could leave. I kept thinking, 'What if the letter was wrong? Maybe Charles is lying in a hospital somewhere recovering from wounds and will eventually come home.' I felt I had to wait. After a time, I realized if he were alive, even if he were not able to travel, surely he would have written. There was nothing, no word."

"From time to time, letters would arrive from Jim, telling about their new life. They had a rough time in the beginning, getting the land ready and a roof built over their heads. However, they managed. Then two grandchildren were born, first a boy followed by a girl. I tried to imagine what they might look like from the details provided in the letters. When a letter arrived asking me to consider coming west to be with them, it set me to thinking. Jim said they could build on a room if I wanted to stay with them, or, if I wanted my own place, there was a homestead near them with a cabin (that could be seen from their place) where a neighbor had decided to move back east. The more I thought about it, the more I asked myself what was keeping me. The memories in my house, depending on my mood, were either comforting or depressing. I was lonely. There were no relatives in the area where I lived, even though there were friends. However, I felt like I no longer belonged. My husband and I had always interacted as a couple to visit friends or invite them over to our place. Now old friends seemed polite and expressed sympathy to my loss, but no longer did we seem to have any common ground. I decided if I didn't go west, I would always wonder if I should have."

"Once I'd made up my mind, things progressed rather quickly. A neighbor had always coveted our place because of the good supply of water from our spring. We always had water even when other people were hurting in drought times. It wasn't too hard to agree on a fair price. The hardest part for me was to decide what to keep and what to part with in the house. Some of the things I was the most sentimental about I realized would be foolish to try to transport on a wagon."

"When I wrote Jim that I had decided to leave Iowa, he sent me a list of what I would need to stock the wagons for the trip. I bought two wagons. There was a man who lived nearby who raised and trained mules. I purchased two good teams. I hired a young man to travel with me to drive and to help, so I felt pretty confident when we pulled out of the Brewsters' lane onto the main road. That last look at the house and all that had been home for so many years was oh so very hard, but I was on my way to see my grandchildren!"

"As I look back, it seems amazing that everything went so smoothly. Actually, I never had any real problem until I crossed the Des Moines River. Even then it was only little aggravating things here and there. The first real trouble was when the young man I hired just up and left during the night without a word. He had seemed fascinated one evening by stories told around the fire by a group of men who dropped in on our camp at suppertime and who were heading west. They said they were on their way to the goldfields to make their fortune. In the morning, the men were gone, and so was my young driver. Mr. McMasters about had a fit when he realized Billy was gone. At first he said he was leaving me at the first town we came to, as he wasn't going to have a woman slowing his wagons down and therefore putting everyone in danger out on the open prairie. I told him I was perfectly capable of caring for the teams. I would find someone to drive the other team. The pastor came to my aid and promised to keep an eye to checking over my wagons and harnesses to avoid a breakdown. Then Gilbert Grayson's father offered to let Gil drive one of the teams. Finally, Mr. McMasters backed off and said something like it was against his better judgment, but he would let me continue. The rest I guess you know."

Sallie paused. "I'm sorry. I've run on and on. Please forgive me for rambling. You asked one little question, and here I am telling practically my whole life story."

Truman found he could empathize with Sallie's feelings and reasons for moving on and not being able to continue to live with memories of the past haunting the present. At least she had her son and family. He had no one and seemed destined to wander forever alone.

He had been standing beside her, leaning against a wheel of the wagon as she told her story and intently listening to every word.

"Mrs. … Sallie, don't apologize. I'm glad you told me. I guess I can understand how you feel about trying to leave memories behind. Only sometimes they follow you wherever you go."

"What happened? What memories haunt you?" He looked up, startled by her question. She continued, "You said you know how I feel."

"Oh, it was a long time ago. I don't know … It's a long story."

"You were kind to listen to me. I'd really like to know, if I'm not prying too much."

"You're not prying," he said softly.

And then he told her about Carrie and Amy, the doll in the little bed, the daffodils outside the cabin door, the need to leave, to just get away. Sallie realized how the loneliness had followed him and the memories haunted him to this day. She listened with tears glistening in her eyes, realizing this tough frontiersman may never have opened up to tell anyone these things in all the passing years.

The moon had traveled across the sky by the time Truman finished. They each sensed a kind of bonding and a relationship growing out of their mutual shared heartaches and loneliness.

After he finished telling her about Carrie and Amy and their homestead, although he hadn't told of his life after leaving the homestead and Harley, he stood for a moment with head bowed. Sallie reached out her hand and lightly touched his arm.

"I'm glad you told me."

Truman nodded and looked up, seeming focused on something on the far horizon.

Then, after taking a long breath, he quietly cautioned, "I reckon we had best get some sleep. It could be a rough day tomorrow if the rain comes upon us before we cross the river."

For a moment, they stood just looking into each other's eyes, and then he turned and was gone. Sallie climbed into her wagon and decided to sleep inside tonight. A breeze had picked up, and she thought she could see faint lightning flashes on the western horizon. Even though the day had left her exhausted, sleep would not readily come, as her thoughts dwelt on Truman Garrett.

7

At some point, Sallie drifted off to sleep, only to be awakened with a start by a loud clap of thunder. Ruefully awakened and with senses returning, she realized the wind was rapidly picking up. The canvas cover over the wagon was straining. Sallie was glad it was fastened securely. She quickly donned her clothes and pulled on her shoes. Then the rain hit, starting not with a gentle sprinkle, but with a pounding. A flash of light was immediately followed by an ear splitting thunderclap. She felt for her slicker near the front of the wagon. It was barely visible in the first gray light inside the wagon, and she wondered if it would get much brighter than this today. She was a bit alarmed when the wind began to rock the wagon. In time, the first onslaught of the storm subsided into a steady downpour, and then gradually lessen to a light rain.

Sallie wrapped her slicker around herself and peered out the front of the wagon. She spotted Marta poking her head out from the wagon immediately ahead of hers to have a look around. Marta waved. Sallie returned the greeting and began to climb over the wagon seat to exit the wagon. She approached the minister's wagon to find out the latest. Pastor Johann Schaefer had already been up the line to confer with the wagon leader as to any changes the weather may have imposed on today's travel, and he was coming back now. His slicker flapping around his body in the still-brisk wind gave him the appearance of an even larger imposing figure.

"We need to hitch up and get moving. Want to get to the river before it starts to rise. McMasters figures if we leave now, we can make it there before noon," he announced as he approached the wagon.

"We've biscuits enough from last night for breakfast," Marta assured him. "How about you, Sallie?"

"Oh, I have something. Thanks," Sallie replied as she hurried off through the rain to retrieve her team and saddle horse.

Earlier, before the storm hit, Truman had saddled the grulla with lightning flashes illuminating the sky. Each flash revealed tendrils of white and pink that raced across the nighttime sky and wove through angry black clouds that were boiling and churning above the silent wagons. The distant thunder was becoming louder. The smell of rain was in the air. The storm would soon be upon them. No time for breakfast; he had to get mounted. They had to get these people moving. If they waited too long, the river they needed to cross later today could be too swollen and the current too strong to safely get the wagons across. It might be days before they could cross if that happened. They would forfeit precious time if they had to wait.

Truman had passed by McMasters's wagon as he brought his horse into camp. The man, to his credit, was already stirring, preparing to break camp and get the wagons moving. Upon hearing a horse passing on the far side of his wagon, he peered around to see who it was. A bright flash had revealed it was the scout, Garrett, leading his mustang. After a brief exchange, they agreed it was best to get the people up and moving. The noise of the approaching storm had many of them awake anyway. Garrett would ride ahead and locate the best place to cross. A river had a way of shifting flow from time to time. It had been a season since McMasters had last gone this way. There could be changes, perhaps a spot of quicksand were there was none before. It was Garrett's job to check everything out before the wagons arrived.

As Garrett pulled his slicker around him and mounted, the wind began to pick up. He hoped there wouldn't be one of those twisters with this storm. He'd had a close call with one of those black funnels a couple of years ago.

The grulla was nervous. He snorted and pranced sideways as they started off. They were heading right into the oncoming storm. Garrett was only vaguely aware when the eastern sky behind him begrudgingly allowed a faint gray to begin to creep upon the horizon, because it was about that time that the wall of rain descended upon him with a vengeance. Both he and the mustang bowed their heads with the onslaught of wind-driven rain and continued with difficulty along the hard-to-see trail. One particularly strong gust threatened to unseat Garrett.

⊢≽≼⊣

The mules stood with heads hanging down as they patiently waited for Sallie to fasten the harnesses in place. The wet leather straps had been slippery and awkward to buckle, but she was finally done. With Joe tied to the back of the wagon, she was ready to travel. As she was attempting to climb atop the wagon seat, she heard McMasters giving the signal to start the wagons rolling. Her feet were soaked, the hem of her skirt was wet and muddy, and she felt her blouse sticking to her in places where the slicker had failed to keep out the rain. She wished she'd had time to change, but the wagons ahead were slowly beginning to roll. Soon she realized it would have done little good had she had time to change into dry clothing. As the line of wagons snaked out across the trail heading westward, the rain began slanting into the opening in the canvas. At least the wind had died down considerably from the gale it had been earlier. Pulling the slicker tighter around her neck, Sallie was resigned to driving in soggy clothing with the prospect of becoming even soggier.

By later in the morning, the precipitation slowed to a mist-like rain. Grinder and Henry rode back along the length of the train, informing everyone the wagons should reach the river before noon. Sallie's wagon was near the end of the line. By late morning the wagons reached a bluff overlooking the river and soon began to descend the deeply rutted trail. Even though the river was supposed to be fairly shallow at this crossing, it certainly looked awfully wide. Her heart sank as she surveyed the crossing. Sallie could see Truman Garrett down there in the river. His horse was standing knee-deep in the water. Truman was turned halfway around in his saddle conversing with McMasters, who was seated on his horse on the bank. Truman appeared to be pointing out various potential difficulties that he had discovered in his study of the crossing, and indicating the safest passage. Her attention was needed in steering the team in the descent, so Sallie didn't look out at the river again until they were nearly onto the bottomland that stretched for approximately a quarter mile between the bluff and the river. The sun was trying to break through the clouds now, and the air seemed thick and muggy. The winds of earlier in the morning were but a distant memory.

McMasters halted the train and rode over to the first wagon. He appeared to be giving directions. Soon the wagons began moving into the water following Truman Garrett across. Grinder and Henry had reappeared and ridden out into the river. One of them was stationed out in the river now on each side of the line of crossing wagons. The current appeared swifter than Sallie had realized from up the trail. However, the wagons appeared to be doing fine. It would take a good part of the day to get them all across. The stock would be tired from pulling their heavy loads against the current, so they would probably not venture too much farther today. They would make camp, rest, and attempt to dry everything out. It seemed that no matter how well the wagon beds were covered with tar, water managed to seep in somehow in a crossing like this.

Noon came and went. There was only one wagon ahead of her now preparing to enter the water; then it would be her turn. The current appeared to be quickening, and did Sallie imagine it, or was the river rising ever so slightly? The teams were still entering the water at the same point, but were now pulling out on the other side a little farther down steam than the first wagons had when crossing. Word had been passed back down the line to be careful not to let the wagons drift too far to the left of the crossing line, as the river bottom rapidly sloped downward on the downstream side of the crossing.

Meanwhile, a flurry of activity was taking place in the middle of the river. One of the wagons had bogged down on something after drifting slightly downstream from the original line of wagons. A mother with a small child on her lap sat on the wagon seat beside her husband. A girl of about ten was peering around the canvas top just behind her mother. An older boy was doing the same on his father's side of the wagon. Grinder was on the downstream side of the wagon with his attention focused on finding the cause of the problem. Henry was on the other side. With so many wagons having crossed ahead of them, the bottom had become quite muddy, and it was hard to locate the problem. The difficulty proved to be a large submerged branch firmly wedged between some boulders on the bottom that had tangled in the wheel spokes and was acting like an anchor beneath the surface. Handing the reins to his son, the father pulled a shovel from behind the wagon seat and jumped into the waist-deep water. Using it as a crowbar, he managed to free the wheel with Henry's help.

Suddenly, a huge, partially submerged tree trunk appeared upstream, bobbing in the current as it floated toward the wagons. It appeared to snag on the bottom from time to time. At which time the front most part of the tree would shudder to a halt. The force of the current would then bring the other end of the tree around. It continued in this manner in a kind of sideways summersault.

The people in the river were too focused on their present difficulty to notice the oncoming danger. Garrett, on the far bank, spotted the approaching threat. However, he and others near him who now saw the tree could not make their warning shouts heard above the noise of the livestock, wagons, and river. Garrett urged his horse into a gallop and raced up the far bank far enough so as not to spook the livestock when he fired off a shot to get Grinder and Henry's attention.

Upon hearing the shot from the far bank, the people in the river looked up to see Garrett pointing upstream.

"Let's get this wagon movin'!" shouted Grinder upon spotting the approaching danger.

Henry made a scramble through the water toward his horse, and the other man pulled himself up on the wagon. With a shout, the father attempted to get the team moving. At first the team balked, but then they began to pull and the wagon slowly moved forward. However, in spite of the frantic urging of the driver, the wagon's progress was too slow. The water was rising, and the current was stronger now than it had been for the other wagons' crossing. The tree was bearing down upon them. It soon became apparent they were not going to be able to get the heavily loaded wagon out of the way in time. They had strayed too far downstream from the original line of crossing Garrett had marked. The going just was not good here with the mixture of submerged boulders and soft spots.

Henry brought his horse along side the wagon seat. The mother placed the smallest child into his outstretched arms. At the same time, the father quickly grabbed the girl and swung her over to Grinder. The mother leaped onto Henry's horse. The father and oldest boy jumped into the water, frantically working to release the team from the wagon. Their efforts freed the team at the exact instant at which the huge tree (in the midst of one of its summersaults) slammed broadside into the rear half of the wagon, knocking that end slightly askew. The oldest boy was at the rear of the team holding onto a piece of the harness as the team was freed from the wagon. He was standing in water reaching nearly to his shoulders, but he had been shielded somewhat from the force of the current by the body of the nearest mule. When the large tree struck the rear half of the wagon, the boy caught a glancing blow from the wagon's front corner as it was knocked slightly cockeyed by the impact. The shock caused him to lose his hold on the harness and his footing on the uneven river bottom.

His father, on the other side of the team, couldn't see what had happened in time to reach his son. The boy struggled to get his feet back under him. He was being carried away from the team by the current.

Grinder attempted to turn his horse and go back for the boy, the arms of the little girl behind him on the horse wrapped tightly around his waist. He managed to get his horse maneuvered to block the boy from being swept downstream and made a grab for the lad. He had him! With the boy alongside, hanging onto the saddle, Grinder turned his horse once again for the far bank. The wagon was listing to one side now as it had been pushed to the ledge where the river depth increased. It hung there for a moment before tipping over on its side. It half-floated for a time as some of its contents rolled out and either floated or dropped to the bottom.

In the meantime, the family made it to the bank. The father immediately took the rest of the harness from two of the mules, and with just the halter and lead rope, he vaulted up and rode downstream along the bank, hoping some of the family's possessions would be retrievable. The oldest son mounted another mule and followed. A couple of friends from other wagons mounted up and followed along to see if they could be of help. The mother, daughter, and small child were taken to one of the wagons for comfort.

Grinder and Henry reentered the river to guide the next wagon. This time, the wagon kept up a forward progression, but it also was being pushed slowly off center by the current.

Seeing another wagon being pushed dangerously down stream by the current made up Sallie's mind as to what she was going to do. She decided to drive her team further up the riverbank before turning to enter the muddy river.

"What the hell is that driver doing?" McMasters exclaimed when McMasters saw a wagon being driven parallel to the river.

Then he realized it was Sallie Brewster's wagon.

"It's that Brewster woman. What's she up to now?" In his exasperation, he slapped his thigh, which startled his horse.

About that time, Sallie turned her team and headed them into the river. At her urging, the powerful mules splashed into the water without hesitation. Joe, tied on behind, rolled his eyes and tried to pull back, but his lead rope was securely fastened to the back of the wagon, so in the end he followed the wagon into the river.

Sallie prayed, "Oh, God, please help me get across this river."

"She's going to bog down in that soft spot for sure. We'll have another wagon stuck. Damn!" McMasters was still fuming.

Garrett's reined his mount alongside McMasters.

"Actually, with the current picking up the way it has been, she may come out just right. We probably should have moved those last wagons' a little further upstream from where they were going in earlier. That's a smart woman." Garrett pointed out.

McMasters grunted and turned his horse away, shaking his head, reluctant to admit agreement.

It looked like she was going to make it without mishap. Sallie passed the halfway point without a snag, and the team was pulling strongly.

They were about three-fourths of the way across when it happened. Suddenly, Jasper began snorting and shaking his head violently and then attempted to rear and lunged to one side. Of course, being hitched in place, there wasn't far he could go, but he managed to pull docile Rocky off line with him. Maybe a bee had stung him or there was something in the water—Sallie couldn't tell from where she sat. As Jasper thrashed around in the water, he somehow got a hoof entangled in the harness leathers. In effect, he was hobbling on three feet.

From where Sallie was seated on the wagon, she couldn't quite make out the situation. The mule's broad shoulders obscured her view somewhat, and Fletcher, the mule directly behind Jasper (and closest to the wagon), was between Jasper and Sallie. All Sallie could tell was that Jasper was somehow tangled. It looked like she was going to get wet. She had already passed the point where Grinder and Henry were stationed. They were facing the other way, busily directing the wagon coming behind her. It was a moment before they realized she was in trouble.

Sallie quickly undid the laces of her high-top shoes and pulled them off. She then climbed down from the wagon seat and, clinging to the wagon, made a leap for Foster's broad back. She landed without a mishap on Foster. Now she had to work her way forward to Jasper and untangle him. He seemed to be less frantic now. She couldn't tell whether it was because he really was quieting down or he had himself so tangled now that he couldn't move. Sallie tried to peer into the swirling muddy water around his legs to see if there was anything under the surface aggravating him. However, the water was so stirred up that it was impossible to tell.

Sallie gingerly tried to see if she could work her way in between the mules to reach him. Seeing how high the swiftly rolling water was to the mules and not knowing if there was a snake or something down there, she was afraid to slide completely off and attempt to wade around to his head. Sallie decided to make her move the rest of the way forward by hanging on to Rocky's harness. She didn't want to worry Jasper further by approaching him from behind. It was not easy, as her skirt and petticoats were now soaked and heavy, making any movement somewhat difficult. She managed to reach Rocky's back and get astride. Then she was able to reach over and begin to untangle the now much calmer Jasper.

In the meantime, Truman had become aware of her situation. Her crossing had been going so smoothly that he and McMasters had dismounted and directed their attention to assisting some of the people who had crossed just ahead of her. When Truman turned to look, expecting to see her coming up the bank, Sallie was working her way forward to Rocky. Instead, seeing her trouble, he vaulted back into his saddle and urged the grulla into the water. Sallie was clinging to Rocky's back, reaching precariously over to Jasper's bridle as she worked, unaware that Truman was on his way to her. The last bit of harness leather just wouldn't come up. It must still somehow be wrapped around Jasper's leg below the surface of the water. She had just started to climb down into the water to get to it when she heard Truman's shout.

"Stay put!"

It was with relief that she saw him coming. In another moment he had reached her tangled mule. He made quick work of getting the leather loose. He then reined his mustang alongside Rocky and indicated she was to slide on behind him. Thus he carried her back to the front of the wagon and, standing in his stirrups, assisted her in climbing back up onto the wagon seat.

"You okay now?"

"Yes, thanks, Truman. I'll—I think we can make it now."

She picked up the lines and urged the team forward. The mules, including Jasper, now responded as if nothing had been amiss.

Truman rode along the short remaining distance to the bank just ahead of the lead mules, but he needn't have been concerned. The rest of the way, they proceeded without mishap, and soon they were pulling the dripping wagon out of the water.

From the waist down, Sallie's dress was soaked. She was glad now that she hadn't had time to change this morning after the rain. It would have meant two outfits to wash and try to dry. This wasn't convenient to do when traveling. Attempting to squeeze some of the water out of her skirt, she realized that at least her getting soaked while atop the mule's back had washed out the mud at the hemline.

She followed the rest of the wagons to the campsite. What a day! The animals were tired and so were the people. A few disgruntled voices could be heard as men and women attempted to attend to items that had become soaked when water had seeped into the wagons despite the tallow or tar that had been rubbed on the wagon beds. With wet belongings pulled out to dry, attention was turned to preparation of the evening meal. Soon the smell of supper wafted in the evening breeze.

Mr. Williams, his son, and the men who had accompanied him in the search for the wagon lost in the river returned. Surprisingly, they had managed to salvage a number of items. While the wagon was lost, enough was saved so that the family was not totally destitute. They would be able to continue to their destination in the wagon of a friend. Life would be difficult for a while, but they would survive. They were thankful none in their family had been lost.

The fading twilight revealed how lucky the travelers really had been to cross when they had. The river had risen much higher and was rushing along at a much swifter pace. The wagons would not have been able to cross at all had they arrived any later in the day. The usually wide, shallow ford of the river had become a muddy, roaring torrent.

Sallie hadn't seen Truman at supper. He must have shared a meal with one of the other families. She was exhausted that evening and turned in early. As she was about to drift off to asleep, she was vaguely aware of the soft patter of raindrops on the canvas over her head. With a prayer of thankfulness at having survived the river crossing, she soon was asleep.

8

As the first mist-shrouded light of dawn emerged, Truman Garrett was already astride his newest mount. After checking on the livestock, he'd ridden to a bluff overlooking the river. It certainly was a good thing they had made the crossing yesterday. With the additional rain last night, the river was no longer fordable. They would have been stranded on the other side for an extended amount of time had they not arrived until today.

As it was, McMasters had decided to stay put today, rest the stock, and make any needed repairs to the wagons before moving on tomorrow. But that was only one day. Had they been stranded on the other side, it might well have been several days of waiting for the depth of the rushing river to go down to a manageable crossing level once again. The teams were weary from the hard push to and across the river the day before, and a day of rest would do them good. The grazing was good here. It also was smart thinking to let the men have today to check over their wagons and take care of any maintenance that might be needed. This would avoid delays due to breakdowns on the morrow.

When they did get started again, it would be harder work for the teams pulling their heavy loads along the now muddy trail. The weight of the wagons would cause the wheels to sink into the mire.

The sky was still overcast, but the rain had stopped, at least for now. Hopefully, the fog would lift later in the morning.

Truman turned his horse toward the wagons. Maybe he would stop by to look in on Sallie Brewster before ridding out to check the condition of the trail ahead. As he approached Sallie's wagon, Truman saw that the preacher's wife and Sallie were busy preparing breakfast. Sallie was just lifting a skillet of steaming cornbread from the fire.

The red-bearded minister was sitting on a barrel, rubbing some oil into the harness leathers. He looked up as Garrett approached. "Had breakfast yet?"

When Garrett shook his head, he continued, "Well, climb down. Smells like it's almost ready."

Garrett gratefully accepted the invitation and gracefully swung down from the bay gelding.

Mrs. Schaefer poured Garrett a cup of coffee from the pot bubbling to the side of the fire. Her husband was already working on a cup that he had set beside him on the barrel top.

"Thank you, ma'am," responded Garrett as she offered him the china cup. Before returning to the meal preparation, she topped off her husband's cup too.

Sallie looked up from where she was tending the breakfast fire. Garrett touched the front of his hat with his free hand in the way of greeting. She nodded and then turned her attention back to pouring another batch of cornbread batter into the skillet.

Jeremy had been hungrily observing the breakfast preparation. Upon seeing his new friend, Mr. Garrett, arrive, he edged a little closer to the men, so as to kind of listen in to their conversation.

Garrett acknowledged the little guy with a "Hey boy! You caught anymore critters?"

Jeremy smiled, and shaking his head, replied softly, "No, Sir." He edged a little closer.

"Do you think the trail will be rough up ahead after all that rain?" inquired Pastor Schaefer.

Garrett took a sip from his steaming cup before replying, "Thought I'd ride out a ways to check it out. Looks like it might be clearing to the west. If the sun comes out, it will dry it some. McMasters is smart to wait a day to rest the teams and mend the wagons."

The preacher nodded his agreement.

The ladies indicated that breakfast was ready. Pastor Schaefer gave thanks for the food and asked the Lord to bless their meal and the day ahead of them.

As they were filling their plates, the sun began to peek through the clouds. By the time they had finished the meal, it was promising to be a good day to dry things out.

"You ladies fixed a mighty fine breakfast. Thank you kindly." Garrett touched the brim of his hat and turned to the pastor. "Reckon I'll ride out now and check that trail up ahead." He mounted the bay and rode out of camp.

Pastor Schaefer rolled up his sleeves and gave his wagon a good going over to see what maintenance needed to be done. One thing he wanted to check after the water crossing was to be sure there was enough grease on the wheels for them to turn smoothly.

Sallie and Marta hurriedly gathered up the dirty dishes. They had put a kettle of water to heat over the fire as soon as the meal had been prepared so it could be heating while they ate. Now Sallie, Marta, and little Meg washed and dried the dishes. With three to share the chore, it went quickly.

As soon as they had everything put away, Sallie started checking over her wagon to see what work was required. She also wanted to check on the inside to see if water had managed to seep in through the cracks and dampen anything. Some of the other travelers were already airing out bedding and things that had gotten wet during the crossing. After a time, the tallow that was rubbed into the seams of the wagon bed to keep out moisture could need replacing.

The day progressed quickly with so much needing to be accomplished in such a short time. Men and women alike were bustling around camp with repairs and cleaning taking place.

After Pastor Schaefer had checked his wagon and made repairs, he came over to have a look at Sallie's to see if she needed any help or if she might have overlooked something that needed attention. Both of their wagons were in pretty good shape, it seemed, with just a few items needing adjustments.

Sallie decided to oil the harness after its soaking to keep it soft and pliable. That way it would not chafe the mules or crack and break with the strain as it would if it were allowed to become stiff and brittle. She sat on a crate under a cottonwood, humming a tune as she worked. The filtered sunlight sparkled over her as a gentle breeze whispered through the leaves overhead.

In midafternoon, she decided to take a break and walked out to check on the stock. Some of the older boys were in charge of watching the animals as they grazed. The mules appeared to be content. Joe, her horse, lifted his head to watch her for a moment before reaching down to tear off another mouthful of grass.

If there hadn't been so much to do, it would have been easy to curl up under the big cottonwood and take a nap. Little Jeremy had done just that under another such tree beside his mother, who was darning a pair of her husband's socks. Meg was braiding the yellow yarn hair of her cloth doll. The doll wore a little apron exactly like hers over its calico dress.

After Sallie finished with the harness, she folded the bedding she had hung out to air in the warm sun and placed it back inside the wagon. Her stomach grumbled, and she remembered that they had just nibbled on some cornbread at lunchtime. Sallie decided to walk over to where Marta and the children were to discuss the evening meal preparations. Marta looked up and smiled at Sallie's approach. Just as Sallie was about to open the discussion regarding coordinating a meal between the two families, Grinder and Henry rode up. They had been successful in their search for game. Henry and Grinder each were leading an extra horse that was carrying the results of their day of labor to obtain fresh meat for the train. Grinder had a couple of rabbits on top of a canvas wrapped around freshly skinned buffalo meat on his.

"Mrs. Brewster, we passed Truman Garrett on the way back. He said as how you was partial to rabbit meat, and I might offer these to you." Grinder didn't mention he'd had a feeling he was being put up to something when Garrett made that revelation about Mrs. Brewster's preference for rabbit. When she attempted to suppress a smile, he was sure of it. However, she gave him no satisfaction as to the meaning.

"Why, thank you, Mr. Gibbons. I'm sure those will cook up nicely. We sure do thank you for supplying us with fresh meat. You and Mr. Laurens are welcome to join us for supper."

"Thank you kindly, ma'am. Me and Henry will just pass the rest of this here meat around and see you all later."

After distributing the fresh kill to Mrs. Brewster and Mrs. Schaefer, Grinder touched the front of his hat and backed his horse before turning it toward the next wagon. The docile pack horse followed along behind his roan-colored one to the next stop. Henry nodded to the ladies and followed along behind with his extra horse in tow, which was also loaded with fresh meat.

"So, you like rabbit?" Marta probed, wondering how it was that Mr. Garrett had perceived this bit of information in his short time with the wagons.

"Well, uh … yes, I guess." Sallie was reluctant to share, even with her friend, the events of a couple of mornings previous. "Do you think we should fix those potatoes tonight?" she said, successfully attempting to divert the course of the conversation.

"That sounds like a good idea. We could make a nice stew with those, and I have carrots and onions to contribute."

Meg joined them. She was given the job of preparing the carrots.

Jeremy played nearby with the wooden soldiers his father had given him. His soldiers were fighting imaginary battles in the grass. A few stones were arranged to form a fort.

Marta's husband brought in a welcomed armload of wood. He and some of the other men and boys had ridden some distance along the tree-lined river to gather what was to be had. Previous travelers, who had camped at the river crossing, had picked the ground clean of firewood in the immediate area. They didn't want to dig into their precious supply of buffalo chips in the sling under their wagons if there was the possibility of other fuel within a reasonable distance.

Pastor Schaefer soon had a steady fire going beneath the iron kettle that hung from an iron pole supported on either end by a tripod-type support. It was only a short time before the liquid bubbled inside the kettle as the meat, vegetables, and seasonings were added to make the stew. It would be allowed to cook for the rest of the afternoon. This somewhat leisurely time to prepare the meal was not the norm. After a long day of travel, they usually had to hurry to get a meal prepared before dark. The ladies appreciated not having to rush. The aromas mingled and wafted though the camp from the many individual family meals being prepared.

As suppertime drew near, Sallie wondered about Truman. She hadn't seen him ride into camp. Not wanting to appear overly concerned about the man's whereabouts, she did not question Mr. Gibbons or Mr. Laurens when they returned. She kept scanning the horizon for any sign of him. Surely he hadn't ridden in without her noticing.

Marta noticed Sallie's distraction without comment.

Sallie mixed up a batter for dumplings and dropped spoonfuls on top of the bubbling stew. To these men, used to simple fare, a meal like this was something really special to be enjoyed. When the meal was ready to dish up, Pastor Schaefer asked God's blessing on their food, and the hungry group filled their bowls with stew.

After the meal, the men gathered over to one side of the fire to continue their discussion about the prairie ahead and what to expect in the mountains further west. The ladies began clearing. Sallie scanned the horizon once more.

Marta quietly suggested, "We can set this kettle to one side of the fire to keep it warm while we heat water for dishes. Maybe Mr. Garrett will be back before long."

Sallie felt a little embarrassed that Marta had noticed her vigilance. She nodded.

Twilight was upon them when a lone rider appeared, approaching along the trail toward the wagons. Sallie knew from the now familiar way the rider sat his horse who it was long before she could see his face.

Seeing her standing out from her wagon watching him as he rode in, he walked his horse over to her.

"Evening, ma'am."

"I've kept some stew warm for you."

"Much obliged, ma'am. I need to speak with McMasters and take care of my horse. I'll be back shortly."

The twilight had deepened into darkness by the time he returned. Sallie handed him a bowl of steaming stew and began to wash out the last kettle.

After a few bites, he paused, gave her a sideways glance, and smiled. "Old Grinder gave you some rabbits?"

"Yes, and he said you had told him I was partial to rabbit meat."

Truman chuckled to himself and continued to eat.

Tonight, after finishing his meal, Truman didn't linger. Tomorrow was going to mean an early start for all of them.

"Thank you, ma'am. That surely was good. I do appreciate your keeping it warm for me."

He carried the kettle to her wagon and placed it in its usual spot.

"Thank you, Truman."

They stood for a moment illuminated by faintly flickering firelight. Then Truman touched the front of his hat, turned, and walked into the shadows. Sallie watched him disappear into the darkness. With a sigh, she pulled her shawl more tightly around her shoulders. She looked around one last time to see if there was anything she had neglected to put away before climbing into the wagon.

9

Stars were just beginning to grow pale on the eastern horizon when Sallie opened her eyes. She had been dreaming she was back on the homestead in Iowa, supper was ready, and she was calling the family to come eat. No one answered her, so she walked out in the yard, continuing to call their names and wondering where they all were. She lay there a moment trying to distinguish between dream and reality. Slowly her eyes made out the ribs supporting the canvas overhead and the shadowy shapes of trunks and boxes stacked around her small, cramped sleeping space on the board floor of the wagon. Wishing she could lay there a little longer snuggly wrapped in her quilt comforter, she made the effort to crawl out from beneath its warmth. She felt for her shoes and shawl in the dark interior. Peering out through the canvas at the still starlit sky, Sallie wondered what new experiences today's travel would bring. She asked for God's protection and guidance through the day ahead. Could her son, at this very moment, be looking at these same stars? Sallie asked God to bless Jim and his family and to keep them safe in body, mind, and spirit. She took the time to pray specifically for each member of the family. Oh, how she longed to be with them.

Everything was so quiet; Sallie thought the rest of the camp must still be sleeping. Pulling her shawl more tightly around her shoulders to guard against the chill in the predawn air, she tied the ends together in a knot in front to keep it in place as she climbed down from the wagon. She would get her bucket and walk down to a little clear stream of water she had noticed yesterday flowing down the hillside toward the river below. She wanted fresh water to wash her face and brush her teeth. Sallie had filled her barrels on the wagon yesterday, but didn't want to disturb any of that supply, thinking she ought to save it for traveling in case they had a dry camp tonight. It was still too dark under the trees to find her way safely down to the stream over the root- and rock-strewn path. Feeling for her lantern, it was soon lighted. Sallie picked her way along the path to the tiny runoff stream emptying its clearer contents into the river's muddy water. The water sparkled in the light from the lantern she set on the ground nearby. Kneeling beside the little stream, she pulled the cloth-wrapped, rose-scented soap from the pocket of her dress. After unwrapping the soap, she dipped the washcloth into the stream and wiped the sleep from her eyes. She wished for a tub full of water in which to bathe. Oh well. Sallie filled the bucket and set it down beside the lantern. Straightening to a standing position, she pressed a hand to the small of her back and stretched. Trees blocked her view to the east, but the darkness seemed to be lifting. Picking up the lantern and bucket, she made her way back up the incline to her wagon. She would prepare a fire for coffee.

Truman awoke in the predawn hour. He rolled out of his blankets. Reaching into his nearby saddlebag, he extracted a small pot for coffee. The evening before, he'd laid some sticks in readiness for a small fire so he could have a cup of coffee and be out and about before the rest of the camp stirred. With coffee pot in hand, he made his way along the slope toward a little steam of clear water he remembered seeing running from under an outcropping of the bluff above the river. It might've been spring-fed, it was so sparkling clear. He figured he'd fill his pot and splash some water on his face while he was there, but he wouldn't bother to shave this morning. Making no sound on the wet leaves, he felt his way along in the darkness. He paused when he thought he heard a twig snap somewhere down below him. When no other sound came, he continued making his way toward the little stream.

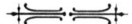

Suddenly, from behind a hand clamped over Sallie's mouth and an arm grasped her around the waist and lifted her off the ground. Kicking and flailing, she managed to reach behind her head and grab a handful of greasy hair and yank—to no avail. However, her attacker nearly lost his balance after a stout kick to the shins from the heel of her boot. In his attempt to keep his balance and hold on to the desperately struggling woman, he stumbled over the lantern she had dropped, tipping it onto its side. It rolled in a kind of half circle with the top at the center, casting whirling patterns of light on the trees overhead before coming to rest against a stone. As he was trying to keep from falling, his hand over her mouth slipped just enough that she managed a muffled scream. The man began to stagger down the dark, sapling-lined slope with Sallie still in his grasp. She was facing forward with him behind her. His left arm tightly grasping her around the waist and his right hand covering her mouth and pulling her head back against his chest made it impossible to determine his identity. Her left arm was pinned to her side.

She kicked out with her feet and tried to wrap a leg around one of the small saplings to slow their progress down the hill. She didn't think it was an Indian that had her this time. She smelled whiskey and sweat and—oh, God! She could hear the river. The sound seemed to rise from somewhere out of the darkness below. They had reached the edge of a cliff above the muddy, rain-swollen river. It ran deep where the swiftly flowing current had undermined the cliff. Fearing her assailant was intending to throw her into the dark abyss below, Sallie now attempted, with her only free hand, to grip the arm over her right shoulder.

"Damn woman. Think ya kin get away with makin' me look bad in front of all those people? Well, ya ain't gonna bother nobody no more. You and yer kin have caused me enough trouble." *The man with the whip and the skittish horse!*

Her captor staggered. Her head was suddenly set free, and the man's left arm slackened enough that her shoes touched the ground. She managed to twist around in his loosened grasp so that she was nearly facing toward her attacker before he gave her a final shove. She was falling. Clawing desperately, she managed to gain hold of an exposed tree root with one hand and a rock outcropping with the other as she went over the edge.

As Sallie frantically tried to crawl back onto the ledge, she was dimly aware of a scuffle going on just inches away from her. The rock outcropping in her right hand began to pull free from the ledge. She grabbed hold at another spot. Sallie managed to swing her leg to get a foot back up on top, and she was attempting to work herself up and over when she heard a man scream. A second scream came from below. Strong hands now took hold of her arms and were pulling her. Fearful, she was reluctant to release her hold on the root until she heard a familiar voice. "I got you, Sallie. It's okay."

Reaching the security of the ledge and rising to her feet, she held firmly onto Truman's supporting arm as she turned with a shudder to look below into the darkness of the rolling, foaming, muddy river.

"Oh, Truman, it was ... Jarrod Larson," Sallie gasped.

Stepping back from the edge, she released her hold on Truman and sat down on the ground. "I don't understand. I just don't understand. Why? Just because I interfered with him beating his horse?" She looked up at Truman incredulously. "And he said something that sounded like 'You and your kin have caused me enough trouble.' I don't understand," she repeated.

Shaking his head, Truman shared his observation. "Sallie, there was more troubling that man then just you stopping him from whipping his horse. You just happened to be handy for him to take it out on this morning, and in his drunken state he was plum out of his head. Talk I've heard around camp is the man always seemed to be angry about something. People kind of steered clear of him."

"You okay?"

She just nodded.

"Come on." Truman spoke softly as he pulled her to her feet, and they started back up the hill, Truman pausing to retrieve his small coffee pot and Sally her lantern, bucket, and toiletries.

When they reached Sallie's wagon, Truman paused. Now that the first glow of morning had chased away the darkness, people were moving about camp busily preparing for the day of travel, unaware of the life-and-death struggle that had ensued so near their peaceful encampment.

"I'll go talk to McMasters; you get your wagon ready to travel."

"What will you tell him?"

Shaking his head as he seemed to study the horizon, Truman kind of stepped around her question. "I'll ride down along the bank to see … don't know … that current's strong right now." Then he turned toward Sallie and his gaze searched her eyes. "You're sure you're okay?"

"I think so. Truman?" Sallie hesitated, at a loss at how to express her gratitude. Then simply said, "Thank you. You must be my guardian angel."

"Guardian angel? I don't think I qualify for that title, not by a long shot." With that comment, he touched the front of his hat and walked away.

Sallie turned toward her wagon. As she reached out to hang the now extinguished lantern on its hook on the side of the wagon, her hands began to shake and the tears began to flow. She put one trembling hand over her mouth and leaned her forehead against the side of the wagon, trying to regain her composure. What if Truman hadn't been out there and heard them struggling? What if? *Oh, God!* It would be her body claimed by the muddy current. God had certainly answered her prayers that morning. When she had knelt in prayer in that predawn hour and prayed "deliver me from evil," never could she have imagined she would need deliverance so soon and so dramatically. What business had she being out here on this prairie? Maybe McMasters was right—she was crazy to have kept going after Billy had left her, or to have ever left Iowa in the first place. Maybe she would never make it to Jim's homestead. Despair threatened to overwhelm her. Desperately she fought to regain her composure. Truman had said to get her wagon ready. What if McMasters came to question her about the ordeal and found her like this? She had to appear in control even if she felt frightened and disheartened. Wiping her eyes with a handkerchief, she took a deep breath and with determination prepared to get her wagon readied for travel.

Sallie hadn't spoken to her friend Marta this morning. The younger woman came around the side of the wagon as Sallie was tying the rear canvas down.

"Wondered where you were this morning. Are—" Marta paused, seeing Sallie's face and the telltale sign of recent tears. "Are you all right?"

Sallie nodded and managed a weak smile.

"Did you hear what happened?" Not waiting for an answer, Marta continued.

"We heard Mr. Larson was drinking heavily, and he and Mr. Garrett got into a scuffle down on a bluff above the river. Mr. Larson fell off the ledge. Mrs. Gorman, whose wagon is near Mr. Larson's, told me that she had overhead Mr. McMasters caution Mr. Larson about his drinking once before. She said she and her husband have thought he had been drinking on several occasions. Anyway, we are going to be delayed a little leaving. Mr. Garrett and a couple of the men have gone down to the river to look for Mr. Larson. They don't think there's much hope of finding him—at least not alive. God rest his soul. Talk is of letting the Williams family put what belongings they were able to salvage from the river into his wagon to use it. Being a man traveling alone, his wagon isn't that heavily loaded. Later on, when they get to a settlement, maybe they can send word back east in the hope of locating an address of his relatives and compensate them or send them his belongings."

Puzzled, Sallie questioned, "You heard it was just the two men, Mr. Garrett and Mr. Larson, down at the river?"

"Yes, that's what we heard. Are you sure you're all right? You look kind of troubled this morning."

"Oh, I'll be okay. It's just that, well, sometimes I wonder what I was thinking to come out here."

Marta gave Sallie a hug, "Sallie, I think you are a courageous woman, and you'll be seeing your son and his family before long. You certainly have been a strength for me. I was so dreading this trip. Your friendship has meant a great deal to me."

"Thanks, Marta, and you don't realize how much your friendship has meant to me." Sallie turned to give the canvas strap one more tug as she tried to hide the emotion that threatened again.

Why had Truman Garrett chosen not to mention her involvement in the struggle with Jarrod Larson?

10

About midmorning, the searchers returned without finding any trace of Jarrod Larson. Grinder Gibbons indicated they had ridden quite a distance downstream in their search. Of course, with the river still at flood stage, it prevented them from crossing to search the opposite bank. The men discussed the situation with McMasters. It was decided, as had been rumored, to let the Williams family move into Larson's wagon. Preparations were soon underway for departure from camp. McMasters wanted to try to keep the group on schedule. If they left now, at midmorning, they could still make it to the scheduled campsite that evening, although it would probably be close to sundown or even later when they arrived. The signal was given to start the wagons, and the lead teams began to move out across the rolling landscape. The deep blue sky was nearly cloudless. It was hard to believe that such a beautiful day followed the tragic happenings of the early morning hours.

Truman Garrett set a pace that soon left the wagon train behind. He needed to be alone with his thoughts. The events of the morning lay heavy on his mind. In the struggle on the ledge, he had only tried to free Sallie from her attacker. He hadn't meant for the man to go over, but when Larson let go of Sallie, he had turned on Truman in his whiskey-blinded rage. Apparently, the effect of the whiskey, the semidarkness, or a combination of both prevented Larson from realizing until it was too late his own close proximity to the edge. Truman had despaired that he was too late to save Sallie when Larson shoved her just as he attempted to pull them both back from the edge. Upon releasing Sallie, Larson had turned to confront his assailant and had staggered as he tried to maintain his balance. A poorly coordinated swing at Truman's jaw cut harmlessly through the air to the right of his ear. However, Truman's fist had connected, causing Larson to stagger backward. His boot landed at the very edge. As earth crumbled beneath his weight, Larson realized too late his peril and made an unsuccessful attempt to grab for Garrett. Garrett tried to reach for the man but was unable to gain a secure hold, and Larson ultimately slipped away. It was then that Garrett noticed with relief the small hand clinging to a large exposed root just below the lip of the ledge. He found Sallie desperately attempting to climb back onto the ledge. It had taken some reassurance to convince her to release her hold on that root so he could pull her to safety. She had appeared so dazed and distressed by the ordeal that he had decided not to make reference to her part in the struggle when he later related the incident to McMasters.

The wagons kept up a steady pace throughout the remainder of the morning, with only a short stop in the early afternoon to give the livestock a breather. The people nibbled on biscuits, cornbread, or whatever they had on hand. No time was allowed for cook fires to warm a regular meal. McMasters was determined to make the planned evening stopping point. The rest of the day unfolded without incident. When the wagons finally reached their designated stopping place for the evening, the sun was sliding over the horizon in a final blaze of red and orange. The travelers hurriedly disembarked from their wagons to set up camp and fix supper.

Marta and Sallie soon had a steaming meal prepared. Even with the need to hurry to get everything ready in a short time, they had a tasty, nourishing meal that evening. Darkness was well on its way by the time they had eaten and began clearing away the dishes. Stars twinkled and moonlight bathed the wagons in a silvery glow as they repacked dishes and kettles that had been washed.

Sallie had seen Truman, Grinder, and Henry ride in together as the sun was setting. Apparently, the three had been invited to take supper at the Carter's wagon, as she saw the men assembling at that middle-aged couple's wagon shortly thereafter. Truman didn't look her way. It appeared she would not have an opportunity this evening to question him about his reason for not mentioning her part in the struggle on the ledge above the river.

By the glow on the canvas overhead when she opened her eyes, Sallie realized she had slept a little later than usual the next morning. She reached for the bucket she had set within easy reach on top of the wagon seat the night before and poured water into a basin balanced on top of a box in her cramped quarters inside the wagon. After quickly washing her face with homemade rose-scented soap and brushing her teeth with tooth powder, she let down her waist length braid. Each night before she went to sleep she brushed and braided her hair. That way it wasn't tangled in the morning, and it only required a few quick strokes of the brush before arranging it in the usual bun at the back of her neck for the day.

The day proved uneventful with the usual diurnal activities. Sallie hadn't seen Truman leave in the morning and didn't see him ride in that evening. She began to imagine he was avoiding her.

The next morning it was discovered that one of the families was missing a saddle horse. No one had noticed anything unusual during the night. It was decided the animal must have somehow wandered off. Grinder and Henry followed what they believed were its tracks, until the tracks merged with that of a small herd of buffalo. The men returned to the wagons later that day without the missing horse, but with a supply of buffalo meat for the wagons.

That evening after many of the families dined on buffalo meat, they cut the remaining meat into strips and heated them over very low heat for several hours. Another way they had learned to make jerky was, after cutting the meat into strips, to tie strings on the outside of the wagon and hang the meat in the sun. It took a couple of days to dry in this manner.

It was a dry campsite that night without a creek, so the travelers were thankful for their full water barrels strapped on the sides of their wagons for just such a situation to provide water for themselves and their livestock.

The announcement that the next evening's camp would have water nearby was welcome news for the travelers. Even though they had their water barrels on the wagons, it was definitely much easier with a flowing stream to camp beside. The wagons made good time that day and arrived at the designated spot well before sunset. Their opinion changed as the campsite came into view. Recent rain had left the overgrazed ground soft. The earth was deeply pitted and scarred from recent travelers and herds of buffalo. Fresh dung and flies were everywhere. The women clutched up their long skirts as they descended from the wagons and cautioned the children to watch their step. It had been announced that a buffalo herd had been sighted over the rise. In the absence of the scouts, some of the men and older boys were interested in trying their own hand at bringing in some fresh meat. In their effort to have fresh buffalo steaks for supper, many of the men took a hasty departure from the wagons and turned a deaf ear to the women's complaints. And these complaints were rampant among the ladies at the condition of the chosen site as they attempted to set up camp.

Sallie noticed a grassy level area a little way upstream and decided to investigate for herself. After bridling her horse, Joe, she swung onto his back and urged him along the stream to the little level area about a quarter of a mile distant. Sallie found it to be a much cleaner spot than where the men had left the women and the wagons in their haste to do a little hunting before dark. She rode back and shared her findings with the other ladies. They decided to hitch the animals back to the wagons and to move the camp themselves. The few men who had remained behind were left with little choice but to assist when they saw the women's determination and were told of the advantage of the other site.

Later, when the returning hunters topped the ridge, they were puzzled at first at the disappearance of the wagons. However, their attention was soon drawn to the activity upstream. Most of the men were wise enough not to question the women as to why they moved the wagons. Mrs. Brewster's name could be heard here and there in the ensuing conversations, however.

After meal preparation was well underway, the scouts returned. Truman Garrett was with them. They were greeted with tales of Mrs. Brewster moving the camp.

Garrett figured he'd drop by Mrs. Brewster's wagon later in the evening. First he needed to let McMasters know about the tracks he'd come across this afternoon. It appeared about twenty barefoot ponies had crossed the trail just ahead of them, maybe around midafternoon. The real puzzler was a lone set of shod tracks that were obviously fresher and from a short time later. If a rider was out there alone, especially upon seeing signs of Indian ponies, why hadn't he joined up with the wagons for safety, or if for no other reason than a good meal and some conversation? It was customary for travelers on horseback or on foot who caught up with a slow-moving wagon train to stop to share news in exchange for a good meal. This one appeared to have deliberately ridden around the train to avoid contact.

McMasters sat rubbing the stubble on his chin as he mulled over in his mind the report Garrett had just given him. "What do you make of it?" he finally questioned.

"Well, we need to keep our eyes open. That's for sure. A man can never tell about Indians. I heard Red Cloud's stirred up, but I don't think we need to be concerned this far east. That lone rider is a mite puzzling. Could be he's running from something."

"Well, we'll post some extra guards around the camp tonight. Get yourself some supper, Garrett, and a good night's rest."

After taking care of his horse and cleaning up himself, Garrett headed for Pastor Schaefer's and Mrs. Brewster's wagons. They were just dishing up the evening meal when he dropped by.

The redheaded minister spotted Truman Garrett as he approached and called out, "Grab yourself a plate and join us."

Sallie was filling one of the children's plates and turned to see whom the pastor was addressing. She was pleased to see Truman approaching. He picked up one of the plates, and Sallie piled it high with slices of buffalo steak and handed it back to him. Marta offered him some skillet cornbread.

"Thanks. This sure looks good. I could smell this cooking way down the trail. If a man were lost and couldn't find camp—at least, if it weren't quite where he thought it would be—he could sure just follow his nose."

Truman seemed to be addressing the two children, but paused and casually looked Sallie's way with the most innocent expression. When their gaze met, his eyes kind of crinkled at the corners with his amusement for a moment before his focus returned to the plate before him.

"Truman, what can we expect tomorrow?" Pastor Schaefer inquired, not catching the implied meaning of the scout's previous exchange.

"Well, there's going to be one rather steep, long grade to climb, but the rest isn't bad at all. Don't be surprised if we see a few Indians. Saw some pony tracks. They may ride up to look us over, or we may never know they're there."

Marta was concentrating on wiping an errant bit of food from the front of Jeremy's shirt when the mention of Indians caused her to pause and question, "Do we need to be concerned?"

"No, ma'am, I don't believe they mean any trouble." Turning back toward the pastor, he added, "However, we do need to be alert and keep an eye on the livestock."

After the meal was finished, the men sat by the fire as the twilight deepened into night, sharing some humorous anecdotes from their past. Jeremy's little head was soon nodding as he struggled to stay awake and listen to the men's conversation. Soon his eyes were closed and the little boy was claimed by sleep. The ladies and Meg cleared away the dishes. The ladies sat for a while, discussing their dreams for the future when they arrived at their destination in the western mountains. They talked and shared until the fire died to glowing embers and the rising moon sent tendrils of silvery light streaming through the open places between the few old trees towering over them and bathed the open prairie in a ghostly light. It was time to retire for the night. Truman thanked them for another wonderful meal. The pastor scooped up his little son and carried him off to bed in the wagon. Marta guided the sleepy Meg in the same direction. After bidding them all good night, Sallie turned toward her own wagon and found Truman in step beside her. She got right to the point of what had been on her mind.

"You didn't say anything to McMasters about the fact I was on that ledge with you and Mr. Larson. Why?"

Truman didn't answer immediately. They had taken several steps before he responded. "I felt it would serve no purpose in involving you. You looked so shaken. I felt—well, I just didn't think there was any reason to put you through anything more that morning."

Sallie accepted his explanation in silence. They had covered the short distance to her wagon. She turned and looked up to find his gaze on her. They stood looking into each other's eyes for a long moment. Then he gently reached out and touched her cheek with his hand. He stepped closer, seemed to hesitate then softly whispered.

"I'd better go," he said before turning and striding away in the moonlight.

Sallie wanted to call him back, but somehow a lump seemed to have appeared in her throat and she couldn't speak. Instead she stood and silently watched him go until she could no longer discern his figure from the shadows that seemed to dance and play with the silvery light beneath the trees. She remained motionless until a little puff of a breeze picked up a loosened strain of hair, sweeping it across her face. She reached up to brush it aside and emerged from her reverie.

In her distracted state, Sallie didn't see the shadowy figure slipping between the wagons. Suddenly, upon seeing her, it halted and ducked behind one of the wagons, and then cautiously peered around a corner to see if it had been detected. When certain it had not been, the shadow again began to move.

Sallie climbed into her wagon and made preparations to turn in for the night. However, sleep did not come easily. For quite some time, she lay awake trying to sort out her feelings. After the long wait in vain for some word that her husband had survived the war, during which time her emotions were in a constant state of turmoil, she had finally felt at peace with the decision to travel west to be near her son. Now she felt so confused. It just had not occurred to her that someone might come into her life at this point in time or that she would feel attracted to someone. What she thought she had seen in his eyes when he had reached out to caress her cheek had touched her heart. Then she remembered the caution she had heard before coming out here that there weren't enough women to go around, and that she should be careful. Was she letting loneliness and a fear of this rough and strange environment lead her in a direction she didn't need to go? She must not be distracted from the goal of reaching her destination. Admittedly, she felt safe in Truman Garrett's presence. He seemed so capable and strong. Was it only her loneliness that was drawing her to him? What else lay in his past? He had told her about his early years of marriage, but no mention had been made of his life since that time. What has he been doing all these years? He spoke the Indian language. How had he he learned?

She recalled a piece of conversation she had overheard between Grinder and Henry. Grinder had commented that he wondered if Garrett was still as good with a gun as it used to be rumored he was. Could this man have killed someone? Perhaps she needed to guard her heart. Yet she couldn't forget the look in his eyes or the kindness he had shown her. Sallie remembered the way he patiently took the time to listen to little Jeremy and how obviously the little boy hung on the man's every word. With these thoughts going round and round in her head, she finally drifted off into a fitful sleep.

Sallie wasn't the only one finding it hard to sleep. Truman Garrett was twisting and turning in his blankets on the ground under a cottonwood. "I must be a crazy fool," he said out loud to himself.

11

McMasters had propped a piece of mirror in the fork of a tree branch and was trimming his beard as the first rays of the rising sun began to glow on the eastern horizon. He was soon interrupted from his personal care routine by the approach of Dale Carter and Jake Willard.

"Mornin'," Greeted Dale Carter. The burly Jake Willard just nodded his greeting. The smaller man was the first to state his discovery.

"Noticed first thing this morning some buffalo jerky was gone from the back of the wagon."

Then Willard shared his findings. "Wife put some biscuits in a canvas bag last night so as to be handy for breakfast this morning. Bag and biscuits are gone."

"Anyone else missing food or anything?" McMasters inquired with his scissors poised a few inches from his face.

"Don't think so, but Mrs. Williams said sometime during the night she thought she heard something scraping at the rear of their wagon. You know they're in Larson's old wagon. Anyway, she thought at first it was one of the kids. When she called out to see what they needed, she said everything got real quiet and then she thought she heard movement in the grass near the wagon. She peeked out of the wagon and didn't see anything, so she decided it was just some animal roaming around and went back to sleep. When she heard us talking this morning about missing some jerky and biscuits, she wondered if someone might have been trying to get into their meager supplies or what had been Larson's," recounted Carter.

"Her husband said the canvas ties were loose at the back of the wagon, and he could have sworn everything was secured before they turned in last night," added Willard.

"Either of you hear anything unusual?" inquired McMasters.

Dale Carter shook his head.

Jake Willard explained, "I've been known to sleep through a twister. It takes an awful lot to wake me."

None of the other families could remember hearing anything unusual during the night, and no one else seemed to be missing anything. It was puzzling. Food appeared to be the only item missing. Just three wagons appeared to have been disturbed.

The incident did little to delay their departure. The wagons were soon underway again along the westward trail under a nearly cloudless prairie sky. It promised to be good weather for traveling. In the haste to get underway, no one noticed the figure lurking, partially concealed by some brush, some distance from the wagon train. It waited until the wagons had moved out and the last wagon had disappeared over a rise before turning and hiking the short distant downhill to a waiting horse. Upon mounting, the horse was steered in a westerly direction.

Truman Garrett had saddled up and ridden out at first light that morning. The grulla was rested and eager after having a day off while his master rode the bay. Truman allowed the tall mustang to lengthen his stride into a steady, ground-covering lope that soon left the wagons far behind. When he felt the mustang had run the kinks out, he reined him in to a walk.

Truman had a lot on his mind. He wanted to check the trail ahead to see if there were any more signs of pony tracks or lone mysterious riders.

Also, he wanted to put some distance between himself and the Brewster woman. He'd nearly taken her into his arms and kissed her last night before he came to his senses. By now he had to admit he was attracted to her. What was he thinking? He had nothing to offer a woman. All he had in the world were his mustangs, his gear, and his guns. A woman needed a home and security. Also, he lived in danger of the past creeping up on him. If she knew his whole story, the years after Carrie, Sallie Brewster surely would not be waiting in the evening with food kept warm over the campfire.

Truman decided to leave the trail and ride north a ways. He figured he'd make a wide semicircle that would put him back with the wagons some time in the afternoon. There was an especially high rise of ground to the north. From up there, he probably would be able to look out over the prairie for miles and gain a better perspective of what lay around them. The grade proved steeper than it had appeared from below, but the mustang did not slacken his pace. Finally they reached the crest. Truman was not disappointed. Indeed the view was expansive. Truman dismounted to rest his horse. The mustang lowered his head to the grass, began to bite off the tops and was soon munching away while the man studied the landscape below in all directions to the far horizon. From this vantage point, he was able to see the distant wagons slowly advancing along the trail.

The wagon train appeared to be the only sign of life in this part of the world. Then Truman noticed movement along the trail some distance behind the last wagon. It appeared to be a lone traveler following along from quite some distance behind the train. If it was someone from the wagons, they certainly appeared to be in no hurry to close the distance. He studied the approaching rider for a while and was puzzled when he observed that the horse paused periodically. Truman decided he would circle around behind the train to investigate on his way back to the wagons.

After taking one more look around, he mounted and urged the mustang down the slope. There was a series of smaller hills to climb and then descend as he continued in the general downward direction to the rear of the wagon train. When he was in one of the little depressions between the hills he would lose sight of the train and the trail momentarily. Upon coming out of one such depression, he realized the lone rider was no longer to be seen. The unknown horseman had either joined up with the train or left the trail. Truman decided to ride back along the trail to determine which it had been. With the passage of the wagons and all of the settlers' livestock, it would prove difficult to conclude which were the tracks of that last horse, but he figured he'd just ride back a ways to see if a set of tracks happened to veer away from the trail suddenly. Truman wanted to find out if the rider on the bay or brown horse (it had been too great a distance to determine accurately the color) had just been someone from the wagons or a stranger stalking them. The behavior observed from the hilltop had seemed peculiar.

The grulla reached the trail and Truman reined the horse to the left, the direction from which the wagons had come earlier in the day. After riding for close to half a mile, a set of tracks turned off diagonally across the others and led off across the prairie and over the crest of a hill. It appeared the rider was skirting around the train to the south. Judging from the increasing space between the tracks, it appeared the horse had picked up the pace after leaving the trail. The animal was shod. Could someone from the wagons be out riding around? It just didn't make sense. Truman continued to follow the tracks. Upon topping a small hill, he paused to look around. In the distance, he could see the wagons slowly progressing. But that was the only movement he could see. It was almost as if the rider had disappeared into thin air. A little farther on, while crossing some rocky ground, the tracks vanished completely. Truman halted the mustang and stepped down. Leading his mount, he searched the earth for some sign of recent passage. Nothing.

Truman took one final look around before turning to mount up again. It was as he was reaching for the stirrup that his eye caught sight of the freshly chipped corner of a stone. Stepping back down he walked over to the spot and squatted down. In studying the ground nearby, he was soon able to discern some sign on the hardened earth. A few broken strands of grass were visible now to the trained eye. From the direction of their fall, he was able to determine the course to follow. Once again Truman mounted and moved out at a walk. Leaning forward to one side of his horse, he concentrated on the faint trail, looking up from time to time to keep his bearings and to watch for the rider. The tracks led down into a small depression in the gently rolling hills. The ground was softer here and the tracks easier to follow. Surely he wasn't too far behind the rider now.

Suddenly some startled birds took flight over to his left. As he turned his attention in that direction, he heard a shot, and something that stung like fire burned across his shoulder. He dove for the ground. A second shot kicked up dirt near Truman's face, and the grulla bolted. Drawing his weapon, he got off several shots in the general direction of the assailant, at the same time crawling, Indian style, into a thicker stand of grass that would offer better concealment. Then there was silence. He lay with his body pressed to the ground, waiting, listening, not wanting to give away his position. The burning sensation in his left shoulder indicated its need for attention and was a reminder he might not be in any condition for hand-to-hand combat.

As he lay with his ear to the ground, listening, he heard the sound of muffled hoof beats departing. They were replaced by the louder thunder of approaching ones. Truman quickly replaced the used shells in his pistol and turning on his side attempted to raise his head just enough to see through the tall grass.

With rifles ready, Grinder and Henry topped a rise of ground. They reined to a halt, not seeing anyone.

"There's True's horse," observed Grinder as he spotted the mustang nervously fidgeting some distance away.

"Over here!" Truman called as he attempted to rise. He looked carefully around as he did so. Even though he had heard the sound of his attacker's retreating horse, he was still cautious.

Grinder headed his mount in Truman's direction while Henry made his way over to retrieve the still somewhat spooked mustang.

"Damn, you've been hit!" observed Grinder as he approached and swung down from his horse.

"Just nicked the fat. Looks worse than it is," responded Truman as he pulled at the torn buckskin sleeve to try to get a better look. It was bleeding profusely, however.

"Was it an Injun?"

"Don't think so. Didn't see him up close. From up on that high ridge to the north, I spotted a rider following the train who was acting a bit suspicious, so I thought I would check him out. Guess he wasn't in a mood to talk."

Grinder pulled a piece of cloth from his saddlebag and attempted to tie off the wound to stop the bleeding.

Henry rode up with Truman's horse in tow. "You okay?"

Truman nodded.

Speaking now to Grinder, Henry said, "You reckon that could've been the same stranger that snuck into camp last night and stole the grub?"

Truman looked up, surprised. It was the first he had heard of that incident. "Someone was in camp stealing food last night?"

"Yeah, two families was missin' … I think it was biscuits and jerky, and Mrs. Williams said she heard somebody tryin' to get into the back of their wagon, but she let out a holler and scared 'em away."

"You okay to ride?" asked Grinder.

Garrett nodded. Henry handed him the mustang's reins. Holding his left hand close to his chest, Garrett reached up with his right to grasp the saddle horn, and, stepping into the stirrup with his left foot, he mounted a bit awkwardly.

Grinder waited to be sure Garrett was mounted before climbing astride his own saddle.

They set a course toward the wagons with all three men warily watching the surrounding prairie. By the time the men had caught up with the wagons, Garrett was beginning to feel a bit lightheaded.

McMasters, seeing the men approaching and Garrett's arm wrapped, signaled a halt for the wagons and rode out to meet them. Briefly, the men explained what had transpired.

"Well, we have several more hours of daylight, and we'll make our planned camp if we keep moving. Garrett, looks like that arm needs some attention."

"We'll see to him," stated the preacher.

He had approached with Mrs. Brewster beside him. They walked on either side of Garrett's horse back to their wagons. Pastor Schaefer reached up to steady Garrett who dismounted a bit shakily. The bullet had cut a path along the outside of Truman's shoulder, making a nasty looking wound. It was painful, but would not affect the use of his arm when healed. However, the bleeding needed to be stopped. The wound needed to be cauterized. A small fire was quickly built. Even with the offered whisky in the hope of dulling his senses, this procedure proved to be as painful as the initial injury. However, with the expert help of another of the travelers, Dr. Deaver, this was soon accomplished.

"I have room for him," Sallie stated firmly.

A somewhat delirious Truman was assisted to her wagon and soon settled on quilts. His horse was tied beside Joe at the rear, and shortly thereafter, the wagons began to roll once again. Sitting on the wagon seat, Sallie often turned to check on him, but he appeared to be dozing.

Upon reaching the campground, Grinder and Henry came to see what they could do to help. They unhitched the mules for her and led them to water so Sallie could focus her attention on Truman. The latter seemed a little disoriented when he briefly opened his eyes before drifting off to sleep again. He drifted in and out of sleep all night with Sallie keeping watch beside him. The lantern was kept lighted so she could see to assist him if the need arose. Sallie had packed some bedding behind her to lean upon, and although she did her best to remain alert, she too drifted to sleep from time to time. Toward morning, Truman opened his eyes to find her still sitting beside him on the quilt-covered wagon floor.

"You need to get some rest. Every time I've opened my eyes, you've been sitting there watching me."

Sallie just smiled and said softly, "It's my turn to watch over you for a change."

He smiled and closed his eyes.

Reaching out, she touched his brow. There was no sign of fever. Hopefully, the efforts of the day before and her care would be sufficient to ward off infection.

At her touch, he again opened his eyes.

"Can I get you anything? A drink of water, maybe?"

He just shook his head and closed his eyes. "Get some rest."

12

Sallie remained beside him until the eastern sky took on the first glow of morning. Then she quietly slipped out without disturbing his sleep, or so she thought. However, he was aware of her movement and partially opened one eye as she departed.

After taking care of her personal needs, Sallie began to pull out some things to make a quick breakfast. Meg and Jeremy scampered over.

"Is Mr. Garrett going to be okay?" inquired Meg.

"I believe he is," Sallie assured them.

"He's my friend," stated Jeremy.

At their mother's call, off they ran.

Before walking over to join in breakfast preparation with her friend Marta (as had become the custom), Sallie climbed onto the wagon seat and peered into the wagon in order to check on Truman one more time. He appeared to be sleeping peacefully, so she continued over to the Schaefers'.

Marta was already busily preparing the dough for breakfast biscuits. With a flour-covered hand, she reached up to brush a stray strand of blond hair from her brow.

"How's the patient?" Marta inquired at Sallie's approach.

"He's sleeping now, and there's no sign of fever."

When the food was ready, Sallie fixed a plate for Truman and headed back to her wagon. She found him awake and sitting up.

"Thought you might be hungry."

"Yes, ma'am, I am. Thank you."

He seemed much improved, to her relief. With his good hand, he reached for the plate of food she carried. Resting the plate in his lap, he seemed able to manage by himself, so Sallie moved to leave.

"You fixed the hole in my shirt. Thank you."

"You're welcome. I did that while you slept last night."

Again, she turned to go, but paused and asked, "Truman … did you see who shot you?"

"No."

"Do you suppose it was the same man who took food from a couple of the wagons the night before last?"

"Could be."

"Do you suppose he is still out there?"

Truman took a sip of coffee before answering her.

"It's hard to say. Now that he knows we know he's out there, maybe he's moved on. Or it could be there's something he's interested in on this wagon train. Just be sure to stay close to your wagon. I don't think he'll try to come into camp again if he's still around."

He handed the empty plate and cup to Sallie and attempted to rise, bracing himself on a nearby crate.

"Think I need to stretch my legs. Where's my boots?"

Sallie set them in front of him, and he grasped each top with his right hand and stuffed his feet down into them. Then Sallie climbed down from the wagon, followed by Truman.

Upon reaching the ground, Truman stood for a minute with his hand braced on the wagon for balance until the sudden spinning sensation in his head stopped. He was surprised by how weak he felt. Well, he'd have to shake it off. He needed to regain his strength and get back out there to look around. He was more worried than he let on to Sallie about the stranger. He was beginning to wonder if there was a connection between the lone set of tracks he'd told McMasters he'd spotted several days ago and this rider. If so, there was more than just stealing some food on this guy's mind. Last night, during one of Truman's wakeful periods, it had occurred to him that, from a distance, the stranger's horse was about the color of the one that had turned up missing a week ago. However, he knew he was in no shape to climb astride his horse today and ride out for a look around. It wouldn't do to get caught out in the open in his weakened condition.

"Are you okay?" Sallie reached out a hand to steady him, seeing his hesitation.

"I'll be fine, just fine. Just need a minute to work a cramp out of my leg."

At that moment, Grinder walked up, leading Sallie's team of mules.

"Well, look who's decided to wake up. Man, you look like hell that's been warmed over. How's the arm?" greeted Grinder.

"Grinder, you sure have a way with words. It's a little sore, as to be expected. Where'd you get that god-awful stuff you called whiskey is what I want to know."

"Jake Willard had it. Claims he uses it to clean the rust off his tools."

"Geez."

"Head a little fuzzy? You sure swallowed enough of it."

While the men exchanged their banter, Sallie walked over to assist Marta getting the pots, pans, and plates from breakfast cleaned and packed for the coming day's travel.

When Truman was sure she was far enough away not to hear the conversation, he shared his hunch with Grinder about the possible connection between the mysterious stalker and the past happenings.

"I'll be." Grinder shook his head as he paused in buckling a mule's harness to spit a stream of chewing tobacco at a clump of weeds. "You really think there's more to this than just some stray buck or no-good thief?"

"I could be wrong, but you and Henry be careful out there. Watch your backs. Let's keep this to ourselves for now."

Grinder nodded. Sallie was approaching, so they didn't pursue the topic further.

"Well, guess that about does it." Grinder gave a final tug on the harness and looped the end of the reins around the brake handle on the wagon.

"Thank you, Grinder. It was kind of you to do that for me."

"Least I could do, ma'am. Figured you'd have your hands full keeping this tall hombre in line. If he gives you any trouble, just let me know." With that comment, he left them.

"Truman, I need to change that bandage before Mr. McMasters gives the signal to get started. Will you sit over here?"

Truman sat down on the upturned wooden bucket, and Sallie began to unwind the bandage. The wound was still oozing a little. Some of the scab that was forming came off with the bandage, causing Truman to wince slightly.

"I'm sorry."

"It's all right."

Sallie pulled out the same bottle she had used for her hands after the incident with Mr. Larson and put a few drops of the liquid on the wound before applying a fresh bandage. The medication stung and had Truman wishing for his own Indian preparation, but he kept quiet. He noticed from the way Sallie expertly treated the wound and rewrapped the bandage that she was no stranger to doctoring.

As they climbed onto the wagon seat, McMasters's voice could be heard giving the signal to get started.

Truman opted to settle his long, lanky frame beside Sallie on the wagon seat rather than back in the wagon on the pallet. This morning there was a refreshing breeze to be appreciated as it rushed along, whispering through the grass and rippling the wagon's canvas cover with an invisible caress. The day promised to be a warm one, and Truman hoped the breeze would continue. He studied the horizon as they topped the first rise. He expected they'd soon be seeing the first hint of the mountains on the western skyline, appearing like clouds on the far horizon. Some people claimed a man could see the mountains on a clear day from a hundred miles away. Truman wasn't sure about that claim, as he had never really taken the trouble to measure the distance himself, but he could attest to the fact that mountains peaks were visible on a clear day at a great distance across the prairie.

Truman watched as Grinder and Henry rode out from the line of wagons in search of fresh meat. He wondered if they would see any sign of his attacker, but doubted they would. He didn't know why, but he had a hunch the guy was still out there somewhere, just out of sight, waiting. But waiting for what? That was the question. What did this mysterious rider want? Why was he dogging the train? It just didn't add up. Truman rubbed his injured arm as he tried to work things through in his mind, but could come up with no possible reason for the recent events.

Could this be someone from Truman's past with revenge on his mind? He was certain there were a few men who would smile to hear he was in the grave. However, those men were, for the most part, the kind who would not sneak around to do it. They were more apt to call him out face-to-face.

However, the more he thought about the attack the other afternoon, the more it seemed to Truman that the ambusher was not as intent on killing him as he was on just not being discovered. If it were someone from Truman's past with a grudge to settle, there had been ample time to finish the job before Grinder and Henry appeared on the scene. There must be something else motivating this stranger to pursue the wagons in such a secretive fashion.

"Is your arm hurting you?" Sallie's question broke through his thoughts.

"What?"

"Is your arm hurting you?" she repeated. "You were rubbing it."

"Oh … no, it's fine."

"Truman?" Sallie paused and adjusted her grip on the reins before continuing. "Truman, what will you do when we reach the mountains?"

When he didn't immediately answer, Sallie thought perhaps she shouldn't have asked.

"I—I didn't mean to pry. I mean …"

Truman shifted his position on the wagon seat before speaking.

"No wonder I see people walking whenever they can. These seats feel like stone after a while."

He paused, that mischievous smile threatening at the corners of his mouth.

"Well, I might just ride on up into the high peaks. Some say there's gold up there. Was told there's a cave up there with walls lined in gold. They say a ghost or spirit guards the trail and that many men have gone up there, but few come back."

"Truman," Sallie interrupted, suspecting he was leading her on.

"Just repeating what was told to me," he insisted and continued.

"They say the ones that make it down from the heights have pockets filled with gold, but they seem to be a bit touched in their minds and can never find their way back to the cave again."

"Well, then," Sallie observed, "that should be reason enough not to want to go."

Truman smiled. "Oh, I figure my mind's already gone, so I'm not in any real danger there."

Sallie just shook her head. It didn't seem she would get a serious answer to her question from him.

Actually, the conversation had set Truman to thinking about what he would do after the wagons reached their destination. He had an old friend living in a cabin near where the wagons would finally come to their journey's end with whom he could spend some time.

Also, McMasters had mentioned there could be some disillusioned settlers wanting to return east. He had mentioned that he knew of some settlers who had chosen land with sandy soil and were having a hard time making a living. Last year the men had said if they had another bad year, they were going to pull up stakes and head back east. If that were the case, McMasters said he would need a scout for the return trip.

It was a shame that some people traveled the long hard trail west, pursuing a dream for a better life, only to discover the harsh disappointment of failure. Perhaps they chose land with poor soil and were not able to raise enough to feed their families. Perhaps sickness or death of a family member inspired some to turn back. It could be for any number of reasons.

Of course, the vast majority stayed. Truman admired the spirit and tenacity of those that did. He understood their desire to have a home of their own and to succeed in providing for their families. He and Carrie had worked hard homesteading their piece of land. Truman remembered sitting with Carrie on their little porch on warm summer evenings and the satisfaction of knowing that together, with their own hands, they had taken a piece of wilderness and turned it into a successful tract of land. To them, it had been their own little paradise. He wondered what had become of the place. Had someone moved in and cultivated the fields again, or had the wilderness reclaimed the land he had worked so hard to clear for planting and pasture?

Sallie had begun to wonder if Truman had nodded off to sleep, as he and been quiet for such a long time. She turned her head to find him staring at the horizon with a faraway look in his eyes. She decided not to break in on his reverie and instead concentrated her attention on the mules. They were ascending a long upward grade. Fortunately, the trail here was free of rocks and deep ruts to steer around. One advantage of being near the end of the line was that the people up front would have already moved any large obstructions found in the way. Upon reaching the top of the grade, she discovered it was a level plateau of sorts. McMasters had decided to rest the teams after the long upward pull. It would be an opportune time to also take a lunch break. They had a quick lunch of biscuits and dried buffalo meat before moving on. Truman opted to walk along beside the wagon for a while.

About midafternoon, Grinder and Henry rode back to the wagons. Seeing them approaching, Truman walked out from the wagons to meet them. Anticipating Truman's question, Grinder shook his head as he and Henry reined their horses to a stop, one on either side of the man on foot.

Grinder turned his head and spat out a stream of tobacco before speaking. "Ain't seen nary a sign of 'em or much else fur that matter up ahead. There's an ox train comin' behind us, though. They must've taken the cutoff trail to 've come up on us so sudden-like. No matter, I reckon as slow as they move, we'll be able to stay ahead of 'em."

Truman nodded agreement to the last statement and turned to walk back to the wagon.

Henry turned toward Grinder, as Truman departed, and in a teasing tone, making sure it was loud enough to be overheard by Truman, observed, "It must be nice. Him jest a settin' up there all day next to that purty widow lady. Ya think maybe he shot his own self, Grinder?"

Truman just chuckled as he made his way back to the wagon.

The wagons were rolling along slowly enough that climbing on board, even with an injured arm, posed no problem.

"Did they see anything?" Sallie questioned as soon as he was settled on the seat beside her.

"No, not a thing up ahead," replied Truman. "

They continued on in silence.

13

As the sun was pushing toward the horizon, McMasters directed the wagons to form a circle for the night.

The cottonwoods usually found lining a stream were absent at this campsite. The nearly level ground just dropped off suddenly to a small stream cut between two steep, five-foot banks. The many wagons traveling the road had worn down the bank near the crossing. Otherwise it would have been difficult to get the teams to water. The lush grass on the prairie surrounding the stream would find the livestock happily grazing tonight.

Truman had led the saddle horses down to water while Sallie managed the team. The horses had had their fill before the hardworking mules were finished, and Truman headed back up the bank. Sallie was about to lead the mules away from the stream when she heard something to her right, just around a curve in the deeply cut bank. Curious, she led the mules a little further upstream, enough so she could see around the bend. All she could see was the stream slowly flowing toward her between the soft soil banks, which were crumbling a bit in places. As she turned and reached to push Jasper's big head around and start back, something sparkling in the sunlight beside the stream near the water's edge caught her eye. She let the mules' lead lines drop for a moment as she stepped closer to investigate. The sparkle was sunlight reflecting on what appeared to be a watchcase lying on the soft, moist soil. Kneeling, she reached to pick it up. It had a pretty filigree design on the top of the case. She had seen a design like that before. Turning the case over in her hand, she discovered the initials C.E.B. carved on the other side. Her eyes widened in shocked surprise. With trembling hands, she carefully opened the case and what she found made her gasp. Inside the watch was keeping perfect time. Opposite the face of the watch was a small, somewhat faded photograph revealing a man, a young woman, and a little boy. Sallie sat down upon the bank with a little cry. She stared at the picture then closed her eyes and pressed the watch to her breast.

"How?" she whispered and opening her eyes looked around.

She was alone, except for the mules standing patiently a short distance away. They were patiently waiting where she had dropped their leads. Was she losing her mind? Again she looked down at the watch in her hand and gently squeezed her fingers around it. Sallie wasn't sure how long she remained in that position, almost in a trance staring at the watch. Remembering ...

The mules stomped their feet, bringing her back to the present. Jasper was growing impatient and began pawing the sand. Rocky stomped a front hoof to rid himself of a worrisome fly.

She carefully placed the watch into her skirt pocket and rose on somewhat unsteady legs. She walked, deep in thought, toward the mules. Picking up the leads of the four mules, she turned to walk back around the bend in the stream and ascend the trail that led back to the wagons. The mules meekly followed her. She did not notice the shadowy figure crouching in a low thicket to her upper left, watching.

"Miss Sallie, Miss Sallie!" Jeremy was running toward her. His foot caught on something in the grass and he tumbled face forward to the ground. Still lying on his tummy, he slowly opened his right fist. With a little sigh, he studied his hand.

"Did you hurt your hand?" asked Sallie, moving in his direction with the mules in tow.

"Berries smashed," responded Jeremy in a disappointed tone, and he held up his purple-stained palm for Sallie to see.

"Where did you find them?" Asked Sallie.

Jeremy pointed toward some low brambles not far from where the wagons were parked for the night.

Suddenly, Meg appeared, coming around the nearest wagon. Upon spotting her little brother, she halted with hands on her hips.

"We'd have enough for supper if you would quit eating them as fast as we pick them," she admonished him.

He hung his head. Then, looking at his hand, he decided to lick the remains.

Shaking her head, Meg turned and marched back round the wagon.

"In trouble again," commented Sallie. It was more of an observation than a question.

Jeremy gave Sallie that little cherubic grin of his, a purple stain evident on his lips and teeth. Wiping his hands on his pants, he climbed to his feet.

"Can I come?"

"Sure. Do you want to ride Rocky?"

Jeremy nodded and Sallie lifted the little guy onto Rocky's broad back. Picking up the leads for the four mules, Sallie led them to where the rest of the stock was grazing under the watchful eyes of some of the older boys. Jeremy wanted to stay to help the big boys take care of the livestock, but Sallie managed to convince him that his help was needed searching for buffalo chips for the evening campfire. Together they searched the ground for the fuel on their hike back to the wagons. Sallie and Jeremy managed to find a few chips. The area near the wagons had already been nearly cleared of the fuel.

"… and she had that man in her wagon!" A gossipy-toned voice could be heard as Sallie and Jeremy hurried between the wagons.

"Well, Mabel, the man was hurt. They had to put him somewhere. He couldn't ride, and she had room."

"I still say it's just not decent."

Several ladies were gossiping as they prepared the evening meal. The others nodded agreement.

Suddenly they noticed Sallie's presence. An uneasy silence filled the air, and the four women, preparing their evening meal, exchanged glances.

Sallie gritted her teeth and kept walking.

Seeing Marta had already begun supper preparations, Sallie told Jeremy where to place their offering of fuel and moved to assist Marta.

Sallie's angry expression and tightly clenched jaw where noticed by her friend.

"Something is wrong," she observed.

"Oh, I guess I'm just too thin-skinned for my own good." Sallie only voiced one of the reasons for her troubled expression. Her hand slid down inside her skirt pocket to touch the other. She was reluctant to reveal her discovery unless she was certain of not being interrupted.

Marta stopped mixing the biscuit dough and paused with one eyebrow raised as she waited for Sallie to explain.

"I surprised the gossip group and found I was the topic of their conversation. They feel it wasn't decent that I had *that man* in my wagon."

"Oh, Sallie, don't let them get to you. It was good of you to help. Most of the wagons are so crowded with trunks and children, the families would have been hard-pressed to make enough room for a pallet for an injured man."

Marta's voice lowered and changed to a teasing tone.

"They are probably just jealous. After all, as I have said before, he is kind of nice-looking for a man his age."

"Oh, Marta!" Sallie sounded shocked that Marta would make such an observation. But then they both began to laugh and the mood lightened.

Jeremy, thinking he wasn't being observed, was cautiously reaching into the pail of berries for another handful when his mother gave him a little swat on the behind with her wooden spoon.

"Jeremy, keep out of those berries, or we won't have any for supper!"

Not suspecting there might be an emotional struggle tearing at Sallie's heart, Marta resumed the meal preparation.

Sallie fought the rising sense of panic as she thought about finding her husband's watch. Before leaving Iowa, she had come to terms with his death and felt she could finally live in the present without agonizing over the past. Now this. What did it mean? The agony of not knowing for certain raised its ugly head to torment her mind again. What if? No, she was not going down that road again. He was gone. The circumstances surrounding his death were a bit questionable or unclear. However, several reliable sources had declared him dead. He died of a wound suffered in a minor skirmish during the war. If it hadn't been for that letter …

A letter had come from someone who claimed to be a friend of her husband's and to have served with him. The man said he felt it was his duty to let her know there was a question in some minds as to whether her husband was really killed by the enemy in the skirmish or shot by one of his own men. He wrote that her husband had demoted one his sergeants for disobeying an order. Since the sergeant disobeyed the command, there weren't men stationed where her husband had directed, and a weakened line during a skirmish resulted. The writer also informed her that the angry man had been overheard later by some of the other soldiers vowing revenge on her husband and his family. The demoted sergeant was declared missing in action after the skirmish that resulted in her husband's death. Then the writer had closed the letter, stating that he'd written because he did not want it on his conscience that she had not been warned of the vow this man had made before his disappearance.

Sallie had written to one of her husband's fellow officers, questioning the circumstances surrounding her husband's death. He had answered, admitting there was a possibility her husband might have been accidentally hit by a bullet from one of his own men as they charged forward over

97

extremely rough terrain—no one could be certain. He wrote that he regretted if knowing this added to her grief.

When she tried to contact the writer of the first letter, she discovered he had been killed in a later battle.

"That sure smells good!"

With a jolt, Sallie was brought back to the present with Pastor Schaefer's comment. She had been absentmindedly poking at the chunk of buffalo meat roasting over the coals.

"I believe it's ready," she responded.

Truman was with him.

"Grinder and Henry are over at the Carter's wagon," the pastor said, explaining their absence.

Pastor Schaefer asked the Lord to bless the food and the evening's rest.

Truman noticed Sallie was quiet and seemed preoccupied throughout the meal. He decided she was probably just tired. She must have been awake a good part of the night, checking on his wound and watching to see if he needed anything.

After the meal was finished and the dishes cleared away, Sallie went to her wagon and pulled out her meager medical supplies. Putting what she needed into a basket, Sallie made her way to where the Pastor and Truman were seated discussing the pros and cons of various types of hay and grain relative to cattle raising.

Seeing her approaching with the basket of bandages and supplies, Truman unbuttoned his shirt. Carefully, Sallie removed the old bandage.

"It's healing nicely. No sign of infection," she commented with relief.

"Thanks to you, ma'am."

The men continued their conversation while she efficiently cleaned and dressed the wound. As she was placing her unused supplies back into her basket, Dale Carter approached the group with his Bible in hand.

"Pastor Schaefer, in what chapter does it tell about the fiery furnace?" he wanted to know.

Soon the pastor and Dale Carter were deep in discussion as they paged through Dale's Bible to the correct spot.

Sallie sighed. She had hoped to discuss the discovery of the watch in private with the pastor.

Truman rose to his feet.

"I'll not need to impose on your hospitality this evening. Thanks to your expert doctoring, I'm feeling fine. I'll just get my blankets and call it a night."

The truth was, his arm was aching, but he felt it best to return to his usual routine. Sallie needed to rest. She looked especially tired tonight.

Truman turned to go. Sallie didn't say anything about the watch. He needed to rest. She didn't want to burden him with her troubles tonight.

Marta was sternly speaking to Jeremy in a low voice. The little guy was in trouble again.

Sallie needed someone to talk to, but there was no one. Climbing into her wagon, she sat down upon the pallet that Truman had occupied the night before and pulled the watch from her pocket. For a moment she sat stroking the case. Then she pressed the case to her lips and kissed it as tears welled into her eyes. There was just enough moonlight filtering through the opened end of the canvas for her to make out the carving on the case. Her hands began to tremble, and she laid the watch in her lap. She leaned her head back on the crate behind her as the tears began to streak down her cheeks. She felt confused and weary.

"God, please help me," she prayed. "I need you to give me strength and understanding. Where did this come from? Am I going mad? In Jesus' name, please help me!" she pleaded.

The watch could not have been beside the stream for long. The case showed no sign of being out in the weather. It was keeping the correct time. Who could have dropped it there—or placed it there for her to find? Sallie tried to picture exactly the way everything had been as she had approached the stream while leading her mules that afternoon. Jake Willard had already been down at the stream. Dale Carter was to her immediate left with his team. Truman had been proceeding directly in front of her, leading his horses and her saddle horse. He had been grasping the leads in his right hand, as his left shoulder was still too sore to allow much movement of his left arm. He had been to her right, but he hadn't gone around the bend in the stream.

The bank was too steep where she'd found the watch to easily lead an animal in or out. Anyone who watered their stock there would have most likely come back around the bend where the rest of the travelers had watered their stock to climb back up to the level of the prairie—unless, of course, there was access further upstream. This was entirely possible. But most people from the train had watered stock as she had done. There had been hoof prints around the spot where she had found the watch. If it had been lying there for any length of time, why had no one seen it and picked it up? She decided someone must have placed the watch there only moments before she found it, but how and why and who? Could someone have been watching her even as she picked it up and opened the case? The thought that someone might have been spying on her as she made the discovery sent a chill through her. She decided she had to go down to the stream at first light for another look around.

Sleep finally claimed her. However, it was a troubled, restless sleep.

14

The silvered light of dawn was still an hour away when Sallie awoke and began dressing in anticipation of her early investigation of the streambed. She picked up her lantern, but decided to wait until reaching the streambed before lighting it so as not to have to respond to questions from another early riser, should she encounter one. Sallie carefully made her way back to the stream.

She was able to find her way well enough until reaching the stream. After descending the relatively low, sloping bank where they had watered the stock the night before, Sallie stood for a moment, looking around her. Apparently, the many wagons crossing at this spot over the years had worn down the walls surrounding the stream. Upstream and downstream, the water had cut a deep groove in the soft prairie soil. Walking just a short distance, the walls on either side of the stream quickly rose to between five and six feet. The moonlight did not penetrate the narrow slit here. Without enough light to proceed, Sallie paused to light her lantern. When she reached the place where she had found the watch, everything looked just as she remembered it from the afternoon before. She decided to walk upstream to see what might be found.

The walls of the streambed became closer together and higher. Sallie felt uncomfortable. The light from her lantern revealed the uneven surface of the walls on both sides of the stream where runoff from sudden storms had rushed over the edge and carved deep vertical grooves in the walls. In some places she could see chunks of earth above her head ready to break away and topple down into the narrow gully below. Her attention fixed on the soft soil cliffs overhead, she was momentarily distracted from where she was stepping along the water's edge, which resulted in a misstep into the stream. It was only a tiny sound, a soft little plunk no louder than a pebble falling into a stream. However, the sound did not go unnoticed. A lone figure reclining nearby quickly unwound from a blanket and silently crept to the edge overlooking the narrow passageway to investigate. Dew on the grass muffled all sound of movement.

Sallie continued along the stream, straining her eyes to see into the near darkness at the edge of her lantern's light for any sign of tracks on the now smooth bank. She halted when she had determined to her satisfaction that no one had ventured along this part of the stream. If no one had approached the wagon's watering spot along the stream from this direction, either she must have missed where they had descended the bank or it was someone from the wagons. *Who could be doing this?* she wondered. *Why?* Sallie slipped a hand into her pocket to touch the cold metal of the case in an attempt to reassure herself of her sanity. She was feeling a mixture of fear and anger at the unknown person or persons doing this to her.

As she turned to retrace her steps along the stream, a soft covering dropped over her head. As her hands shot up instinctively to ward it off, a shadowy figure sprang from above. The attacker's weight crushed Sallie to the ground. The air seemed to have been knocked from her body by the blow, and when she tried to gasp for replacement, the tightly wrapped covering about her head made it so difficult that she feared she would suffocate. Her wrists and ankles were quickly bound. The suffocating covering wrapped about her head was loosened and she was able to gasp enough air to attempt a scream. That was a mistake. A hand quickly slid under the blanket and stuffed a rag into her mouth. Afterward, the blanket was again tightened about her head. She was yanked to her feet, tottering for a moment before she was picked up and carried for a short distance.

Her captor was now apparently climbing out of the gully. He was grunting with the effort of the ascent, half carrying and half dragging her along. Reaching level ground, she was shoved to the ground. Helplessly, she was forced to lie there listening to faint rustlings as he apparently broke camp. Then the faint soft thud of a horse's hooves approaching across the grass could be heard. She was yanked to her feet, the rope binding her feet was untied, and she was hoisted into a saddle. Her bound wrists were further secured to the horn of the saddle and someone climbed aboard behind her. Her captor's left arm was at her side, apparently holding the reins to guide the horse, and his right hand grasped her right shoulder like a vice. It was hopeless to try to escape. The horse moved out at a walk. With the hood over her head, the gag in her mouth, and a feeling of helpless panic in her heart, she tried desperately to peer through the cloth of the hood to discern their direction or some landmark by which to find her way back to the wagons should she be able to escape. However, it was useless. The weave was too close to see through, and the light of dawn had not yet appeared.

How long would it be before someone noticed her absence from the wagons? Would they be able to find her? Truman … Would he pass by her wagon before ridding out to scout the trail this morning, or would he saddle his horse and head straight about his business? He was a bit unpredictable at times. She prayed he would come by her wagon and, noticing no preparation for travel taking place, start looking for her. If anyone could find her, he surely could.

The horse beneath her paused and then began slowly and carefully descending a steep slope. When they reached the bottom, she heard the splash of its hooves in water. They must have reentered the streambed. Oh, how would anyone ever find her? What was the meaning of all of this? Was this somehow connected to finding the watch or some other terrible fate? Truman had warned her and all of the families not to wander far from the wagons. Why hadn't she shared her finding of the watch and asked someone to go along with her back to the stream?

Truman decided to saddle the grulla. After a day of rest, he would be ready to work again. The left shoulder reminded Truman he'd been injured if he moved wrong, but other than being a little stiff and sore, it really wasn't all that bad. Dr. Deaver and Sallie Brewster had done some good doctoring for sure. Maybe he would go by Sallie's wagon on his way out. It was a little early, just the first lightening of the eastern horizon, but she'd probably be up. Truman had observed that she was usually one of the first women moving about in the morning.

He was a little surprised to see no sign of her stirring as he approached her wagon. But then he remembered how tired she had looked the night before. Maybe she had wanted to sleep in until the sun started to creep over the horizon. He wouldn't disturb her rest. Truman rode on by her wagon without pausing. He decided he would water his horse and splash some water on his own face before heading out to scout the trail. A little coffee would have been nice, but not many people were up this early and no one he'd noticed had even started a fire. He'd do okay.

He chuckled a little to himself at the thought. He was getting soft traveling with these kind folks. They were always ready to share what little they had as they traveled into this unfamiliar land. Would many of them have come west if they truly realized what hardships—and, for some, heartbreak—lay ahead of them? He thought of little Jeremy and Meg. Would their parents be successful with the dream of building a new life in the West? He felt so much depended on chance. He and Carrie seemed to have everything going for them and then the dream had died. He hoped that it would not be the same for the Schaefers. Pastor Schaefer was a good man. Truman sensed a confidence and conviction in the pastor that he wished he had.

The grulla descended the slope to the stream and lowered his head to drink. Truman scanned the gray, shrouded banks and cliffs before dismounting. Walking a little ways upstream, he untied the scarf around his neck, and, kneeling, dipped it into the water. The cool, wet cloth felt good on his face. He rose to his feet.

The mustang paused for a moment in his drinking to raise his head. He appeared to be looking at or listening to something upstream. Truman studied the horse for a moment. The horse suddenly startled and blew with a rattling sound through his nose as if disturbed by something. Truman reached for the reins in case the horse bolted. Again the grulla blew with that rattling sound. He nervously pranced back from the stream and turned his body facing upstream with head raised, eyes wide and ears pricked forward, listening. Still Truman could see and hear nothing.

There was only a gray light here at the watering place as on the prairie above. Darkness still lingered between the steeper walls upstream.

Truman decided to investigate. As he placed his foot in the stirrup, the mustang bolted forward, causing a sharp pain to shoot through Truman's injured shoulder. However, it didn't prevent the rider from gaining his seat in the saddle. Truman urged the grulla away from the stream and back up to the level prairie. He did not want to risk the confines of the darkness enveloping the upper streambed and felt it would be more prudent to ride along the ridge to study the depths below. Dawn was already quickly dispelling the darkness. If it was a wild animal or intruder, he would be better off above than below. Along the ridge they cautiously proceeded, horse and rider alert.

Suddenly, the mustang shied and halted, eyeing the ground. Truman could see what had disturbed him. The long prairie grass was trampled down here. He dismounted, holding tightly to the reins, as he examined the ground. It appeared someone had left this spot only a short time ago. The dew appeared disturbed in the area of trampled grass and there was fresh horse dung. A piece of torn cloth lay discarded on the ground. Picking up the material, he decided it was part of a towel like material that ladies used to wipe their dishes dry. Further examination revealed what appeared to be breadcrumbs clinging to it. He tucked the fragment into his belt.

With daylight advancing, he could discern there were two trails branching off from this trampled area. One narrow trail led to the rim. It appeared, from the direction the grass was flattened against the earth, that something had been dragged from the rim toward the larger trampled area. The other trail appeared to lead away from the larger area and form a narrow track running perpendicular to the rim. Truman mounted the grulla to follow the latter trail. The eastern horizon was now a bright pink, heralding the approaching sunrise. After a time, the rim above the streambed lowered, and he found that the path he was following dropped down to the stream at this point. It was here, where the earth was without the covering of prairie grass, that he could clearly see tracks of a shod horse. If this weren't an Indian pony, why would someone camp so close to the settlers and not ride on in as was customary?

Unless, he thought, the stranger was back. Had that mysterious rider never really left? Maybe this was a trap being set for Truman to ride into. Could it be someone from his past with a score to settle? His sore shoulder certainly made him think of that possibility. He wanted to follow the trail. However, Truman's first duty was to the wagons. Whatever the reason for this camp follower, Truman should alert McMasters so that he would be ready to take necessary action. He reluctantly turned the grulla back from the trail that led down to the stream and hurried to warn the man in charge of the wagons.

The train was bustling with activity as he approached. Some folks were eating breakfast and a few were already beginning to repack their wagons. He located McMasters, who was giving directions to a couple of the older boys, cup of coffee in hand. As the boys moved away to their tasks, Truman dismounted. McMasters listened as the scout shared his findings.

"We'll just have to keep alert. I don't know what to make of this. Garrett, don't take any chances out there." McMasters tossed the rest of his coffee and set the empty cup on top of his wagon seat. He stomped off to get his team, wondering what the deal was with this hombre following the wagons. Some of the people were starting to get spooked.

As the scout turned to mount up, he noticed the pastor approaching. From the concerned look visible on the man's face, Truman knew it would not be the usual cheery greeting.

"Truman, we haven't seen Sallie Brewster all morning. She's usually up long before any of us. Marta checked her wagon. She's not there. I brought her team and saddle horse in. She's just nowhere to be found."

McMasters, still within hearing, halted and spun around. For a moment he stood speechless.

"We can't hold up the wagons this time to look for her. If that ox train several miles back catches up to us and passes, it'll be hell to pay. That dirty bunch will spoil the grazing and will make us eat dust for days. The trail gets narrow up ahead and we'll not be able to pass them. Those oxen can't move as fast as our horses and mules. Our stock will be in a fretful state. Get Thad Grayson's boy, Gil, to drive her wagon."

Turning to the scout, McMasters continued, "Garrett, you see if you can locate that woman."

As the wagon captain stomped off, shaking his head, fragments of muttering could be heard. Something about "widow woman … the death of me."

Pastor Schaefer and Truman Garret exchanged glances. Then the pastor hurried to locate the Grayson boy and to finish hitching his own and Ms. Brewster's wagons.

Truman tried to decide where to start his search. The last place she had been seen was as she had climbed into her wagon the evening before, so that was as good a place as any. However, the ground was trampled with all the activity this morning. Her water bucket was still in the wagon, but maybe she had walked down to the stream. What if …

He mounted and urged the grulla into a run back to where the trampled grass lay along the rim above the stream. Upon reaching the spot, Truman halted the animal and swung down. The area where it appeared something heavy had been dragged was still lying flat against the earth. Truman decided to go over the rim and down below to the stream. Leaving the mustang at the edge of the rim, Truman descended. He found the descent was not as difficult as it appeared when viewed from above. Upon reaching the stream bank below, he saw what he had feared he would find: the signs of a struggle. One set of boot prints was that of possibly a small lady's feet and the other was much larger. A lantern lay on its side where it had fallen, half-submerged in the water.

Hurriedly, he climbed back up to his waiting horse. Even as he struggled to regain his breath from the exertion of the climb, he leaped into the startled horse's saddle and urged him quickly into a gallop along the earlier traveled narrow trail along the rim. Soon horse and rider came to the place where the mysterious stranger had ridden down into the stream again and, it appeared, had traveled for some distance in its shallow, slow-moving current before exiting on the other bank and up a low slope to the prairie.

The tracks led off to the west and north, away from the wagons. Now, in the bright morning light, Truman could tell for sure that the shoe prints were indeed the same as those following the wagons a couple of days ago. The left fore shoe had what appeared to be a little nick in it. One thing was for certain: the stranger had returned. Was it really Sallie he wanted? Or was he trying to lure Truman out in the open again?

As Truman continued on, the terrain began to slope increasingly upward. Hill country was not far away. If the stranger chose to disappear into the valleys or to ascend the rocky slopes, it would be harder to find them. Truman was hoping that man's horse was not as tough as his mustang. Also, the other horse was carrying a double load. They would have to rest eventually. Truman was counting on closing the distance when they did.

15

THE HORSE HALTED. FOR A moment the rider sat motionless as he surveyed the horizon. Then he dismounted and the hooded and bound prisoner was roughly jerked from atop the horse and dropped at his feet. The horse was led a few steps away, the saddle's cinch loosened, and the horse allowed to graze.

Even though the hood prevented her from seeing, Sallie knew her captor was not far away. The wad of cloth in her mouth, the tightly wound hood and the increasing warmth of the morning sun made it hard to breathe. She tried twisting her tightly bound wrists in an effort to restore circulation to her hands. Suddenly, the rope around her wrists was yanked and a hand checked the bindings. Then she was left alone, not daring to attempt to move again. She was sure from the stinging that the skin on her wrists was torn and bleeding.

After a short rest, she was aware that the horse was being led back to where she sat in the grass. She was suddenly yanked to her feet and lifted to the horse's back. Again they set off. The heat of the day gradually increased.

Finally, they stopped again. By now, the heat was nearly unbearable beneath the hood, and the rag in her mouth seemed to have absorbed every drop of moisture. When she was pulled from the horse's back, she fainted. The bindings securing the hood were loosened and the cloth was removed from her mouth as her captor offered her some water. Regaining consciousness, even with the hood still in place, Sallie was able to see the man's hand and a dark gray patterned shirtsleeve cuff as he held the cup for her to drink. The water appeared slightly muddy, but she didn't care. He must have dipped the cup into a nearby stream. She was relieved when the gag was not replaced as the hood was again tightly secured. Soon they were on their way again.

About midafternoon, when they halted, Sallie at first assumed they were just stopping to rest the horse. The trail had become a winding upward path. She had sensed the horse at times straining beneath her. She could often hear rocks or gravel sent rolling beneath its hooves. However, the rider behind her suddenly seemed tense. He was not dismounting. She could hear a horse approaching. Someone must be joining them.

Something was happening. Voices—she couldn't understand … With effort, Sallie tried to concentrate. The heat had dulled her senses. The man on the horse behind her spoke for the first time.

"How much further to camp?"

A gruff sounding voice responded, "Not far. This way."

The voice of the man behind her had seemed strangely familiar. However, it was hard to place it from just that short sentence.

They began moving again, not realizing that their movement on the upward bound trail was being observed from the prairie below.

Sallie listened carefully for any sound that might give her a hint of where they were. She only knew they had been climbing and that the trail seemed to have leveled out. Even if she could escape, how would she know which way to run? With the hood over her head, she would have no sense of direction or familiar landmarks to use to return to the wagons.

Her captor dismounted and pulled her from the horse. When she tried to stand, her knees threatened to buckle. A hand grabbed her arm and led her a short distance. Then, pressing down on the top of her shoulder, her captor indicated she was to sit. Her hands were untied and then retied behind her back. She sensed she was being tethered to something, perhaps a tree. His footsteps retreated. She was left alone.

Voices could be heard from time to time, but they were not close enough for her to determine what they were saying. It seemed like a long time before she heard someone approaching.

A voice said, "So this is the woman who caused you so much trouble. She don't look dangerous. What you going to do with her?"

"Haven't made up my mind for sure just yet."

Then the bindings on the hood were finally loosened and the hood removed. Sallie was shocked to finally discover the identity of her captor.

"Jarrod Larson!" She gasped. "You're alive! Why are you doing this?"

"You damn Brewsters acting so high and mighty! I'll show you! I'll show you! You won't tell me what to do anymore. No, sir. I'm Sergeant Jarrod Larson to you."

Sallie, getting over the initial shock of discovery and looking into the eyes of this man as he ranted, began to wonder about his sanity. Something wasn't right with him. This time it couldn't be attributed to liquor. He appeared to be possessed with hatred. Anger flashed in his eyes.

"I earned my sergeant stripes. He had no right to take them from me. But I got his watch. I showed you that. After I take care of you, I'll find that son of his and clear this earth of all you Brewsters. He had no right. No, sir. I'm Sergeant Jarrod Larson." With that declaration, he stomped off toward the others in the group.

Sallie sat wide-eyed with the horror of that revelation. Her body trembled with anger and fear. She had to survive and to escape. The letter from her husband's associate! This must be the man he had warned her about. He had not only murdered her husband and was planning to kill her next, but he was after their son as well. *This man must be insane*, she thought. To think he had been on the wagon train all along. Suddenly it occurred to her that he must have been hunting her, tracking her like an animal even before she joined the train. It couldn't have been an accident that they had both chosen the same wagon train.

That morning, after the river crossing, when he had tried to throw her off the cliff above the river, what was it she thought he had said? It was something like, "You and your kin ain't going to bother nobody no more. You caused me enough trouble." Dear God, he wasn't referring to the incident with her preventing him from abusing the horse, but to her husband demoting him during the war. He had to be the stranger that was stalking the wagons. He had been out there waiting, just waiting for his chance to murder her. What could she do? What could she possibly do?

She frantically looked at her surroundings. It wasn't very encouraging. Some distance away, a campfire had been started for a meal. One man was roasting a large chunk of meat over the fire, another sat on a rock cleaning his pistol, and one more was unsaddling his horse. Jarrod had squatted down by the fire and stayed in that position, just staring into the flames. The two men over by the horses were apparently discussing her, as they would look in her direction every once in a while. They were too far away for Sallie to hear the conversation. Beyond them she could see quite a number of horses. There appeared to be more than this small group of men would need on a normal working basis. She could see no wagons.

Who were these men with him? Were they his associates, or just men he had joined up with out here on the prairie? There certainly did not appear to be much comradeship between them. The men appeared to be a dirty and ragged lot.

The terrain was fairly open, with just a few scattered trees on this little high plateau overlooking the prairie. It would be difficult for anyone to approach without being detected or for someone to leave unnoticed.

The man cooking motioned to the others. Apparently, the meal was ready. They all gathered quickly around the fire. The man who had been cleaning his gun brought her a plate of meat and a cup of black coffee. Setting the cup and plate down, he untied her hands and retied them in front of her so that she could manage to eat. However, he still secured one end of the rope to the tree. He didn't respond to her thanks for the meal. Sallie was thirsty but would have to wait for the coffee to cool.

The men sat around the fire talking. At least the other four men did. They would glance her way every once in a while. Jarrod Larson appeared to just sit and stare into the fire. He seemed to have totally dismissed any thought of her. Long after darkness had descended, the man who had brought her the food came to retrieve the cup and plate. He changed her bindings once again. This time her hands were tied behind her with the small tree to her back. This done, he returned to the fire without a word. Sallie remained tethered to the tree. The fire was burning low. She tried to work the knots at the tree but couldn't get her fingers to loosen them. Hopelessness filled her heart.

She was exhausted, but somehow she had to manage to escape. Her life and that of her son depended on it. She prayed. At some point, she must have dozed. Sallie awoke with a start and noticed the fire was down to just embers. A coyote was howling in the distance, so she assumed that must have been what had awakened her. Again, she tried to work the knots on her bindings. Her cold, half-numb fingers were still having no luck. Suddenly, she heard a sound in the grass behind her, and as she startled at the sound, a hand covered her mouth.

"It's okay. Keep down," came the whispered command.

Tears of relief sprang into her eyes as she recognized the voice.

She could feel her bindings being cut.

"Wait here for me by this tree. Be ready. I'll come for you."

He then disappeared so silently and completely into the darkness that in her exhausted, half-awake state she almost wondered if she had imagined his presence. Looking down at her hands, she saw that they were indeed free. This was real. He had come for her.

"Oh, dear God, please help us to escape," she prayed.

It seemed an eternity of waiting and wondering. Where was he?

Suddenly, gunfire erupted from the other side of camp. A pounding could be heard as horses began to stampede. The sound was becoming louder. The ground trembled. The frightened animals were heading in the direction of the camp. The sleeping men awoke with a start and jumped to their feet, grabbing boots and guns in a desperate attempt to flee.

Jarrod Larson jumped to his feet, gun in hand. A rider was bearing down upon him in the silvery-lighted darkness. As Larson tried to take aim on the approaching rider, a shadow passed over the moon. His gun roared, but the bullet missed its mark. However, Garrett's aim was true, and Larson disappeared beneath the stampeding horses.

Sallie clung to the tree, trying to peer into the darkness. She could see the flash of guns in the night and prayed for Truman's safety. Horses thundered pass her.

All at once, he appeared out of the darkness and swirling dust, reaching for her from the back of the grulla. She leaped from the tree onto the mustang's back directly behind Truman, wrapping her arms tightly around his body. Down, down, down the trail they raced, the surefooted mustang never missing a step. The trail was steep in places and wound around large boulders. Some of the frightened horses from the camp continued down the trail, eyes wide with fear, nostrils flaring. The air smelled of of dust and fear as they descended. A horse stumbled directly in front of them but regained his footing and continued, causing the grulla only a slight hesitation in his stride. Gradually, the panic lessened and the pace became less frantic. The trail became wider and the few horses that had stayed with them began to slow.

Upon reaching the prairie below, Truman reined the mustang to a walk. They continued on, turning in the saddle from time to time, their eyes searching the trail behind them and listening for the sound of pursuit. Gradually, the darkness of the eastern horizon began to fade into gray.

When they were a safe distance away with no indication of being pursued, Truman reined to a halt to rest the grulla. Sallie dismounted first and Truman followed. As he turned to face her, Sallie reached for him, and he wrapped her in his arms. The embrace felt so natural. They stood there for a long moment, Sallie resting her head against his chest. Then she took a small step back and raised her head. Without speaking, they looked into each other's eyes, searching. Truman stroked her cheek with his thumb and then slowly lowered his head. Their lips met softly and gently. Then the kiss deepened. For a long moment, they remained in each other's arms. Finally, Sallie whispered.

"I should have known you'd come."

He nodded and kissed her again.

After a moment, she took a step back from Truman. Their eyes returned to the trail down which they had fled as it began to be washed by the dawn's gray light.

"Do you think someone will come?" Sallie asked with a shiver.

"Larson's dead. If any of the others survived the stampede, they may try to round up some of their livestock, but I doubt they will come looking for us."

"Truman, Jarrod Larson killed my husband. To think, all this time, just following the train and waiting … watching."

Sallie struggled to keep her composure and continue. She pulled the watch from her dress pocket.

"When I found my husband's watch on the ground by the stream the other night, I began to wonder if I was losing my mind."

"A man who had served with my husband during the war had written to me indicating that the circumstances surrounding my husband's death were suspicious. But this … who could have imagined anything like this? This has been like some kind of a terrible nightmare! How could anyone be so vindictive? Larson told me he was also intending to find my son and to destroy all of the Brewsters."

"Sallie, the man had to be crazy. He's gone now. You and the rest of your family are safe."

"I owe you my life. So many times these past weeks, you have been my guardian angel."

"You've called me that before. Believe me, I'm probably the last man God would want to use as a guardian angel."

"Oh, Truman, don't be so sure. Don't be so sure."

They stood for another moment, looking into each other's eyes.

Truman, feeling uncomfortable with the emotions stirring in his heart, turned to tighten the saddle's cinch. As he did, his eyes scanned the distant horizon once again for any sign of pursuit.

"Truman?" she haltingly started.

At the sound of her voice, he turned toward her.

How could she tell him her feelings? Suddenly it felt like her heart was stuck in her throat, but at the same time she felt compelled to somehow speak her mind.

Sallie couldn't look into his eyes. She was afraid at what she might or might not see.

"I ... uh," she tried to begin again, looking downward at the ground. Then, taking in a deep breath, she continued. "I think you should come with me ... to my son's. We could ... I don't know ... we ... I ... I can't imagine going on without you."

Sallie paused and was unable to continue.

Truman gently touched her cheek. She looked up into his eyes and saw the tenderness there.

Softly he managed to say, "Sallie, I have nothing to offer you. All I have in this world of any value is this mustang and the bay. You deserve more than that.

"I had thought that mysterious rider might turn out to be someone looking for me with a grudge to settle. There's a chance that kind of situation might just turn up in my life. You don't need a man bringing you more grief after what you've been through. My feelings for you are too strong to want to see you hurt."

"Truman, we live in an uncertain world. Who knows but God how many years we will have on this earth or what will happen tomorrow? We've both been haunted by the sorrow in our past. When I look at you, I see a good man. Sometimes I think you just have to follow your heart."

Gently he kissed her. Then he managed to whisper. "We could make a start."

For a long moment, they stood wrapped in each other's arms.

Finally, he stepped back and mounted the mustang in one smooth motion. Then, sliding his left foot from the stirrup and reaching for Sallie's hand, he assisted her in mounting behind him. Studying the trail behind them one final time, Truman started the grulla in the general direction of where he figured the wagons should be. Cutting across country would be rougher going, but Truman estimated they should be able to overtake the wagons by some time in the afternoon.

16

Pastor Schaefer was just finishing the watering of the two teams, his and Mrs. Brewster's, when he noticed movement on the horizon. Upon closer inspection, he made out what appeared to be a horse carrying two riders approaching camp. Soon, as the horse drew nearer, he recognized Garrett's mustang and realized the second rider must be Sallie Brewster. He hurried to tell Marta that their friend had been found. As the last rays of the setting sun bathed the earth in a red glow, the approaching horse with its double load entered the camp. Friends and acquaintances hurried to meet them. Marta, the pastor, and their children were the first to greet them.

"You had us so worried. I'm so glad you're safe!" Marta exclaimed. As the riders dismounted, Jeremy and Meg wrapped their arms around Sallie in a big hug.

"Knew you'd find her," the Pastor told Garrett.

At the edge of the crowd that formed, no one seemed to pay much mind to the loudly whispered accusations by two women.

"She's been out all night with that man, and they have the nerve to ride back in here just as brazen as you please. What do you make of that? It's a scandal, I say. A scandal it is."

The other woman nodded her agreement.

Truman Garrett briefly told the listeners what had happened and the true identity of their mysterious stalker. There were many gasps of astonishment to learn Larson had survived the earlier incident at the flooded crossing and had such evil intentions toward Mrs. Brewster. After giving only the highlights of the day before, Garrett left to put his horse up for the night and check on his other animal. Pastor Schaefer walked beside him. The crowd dispersed as the other travelers moved off to their own wagons.

"You just sit right there. You look exhausted," Marta called over her shoulder to Sallie as she hurried to check the meal. To Meg, she added, "You give that stew a stir. Careful you don't burn yourself."

A weary Sallie sat down on the prairie grass with little Jeremy by her side. Marta and Meg hurried to check on the stew, which was ready to eat.

Soon, Truman and the pastor returned, and after the blessing was given, the little group of friends began to eat. As the meal was ending, Sallie and Truman exchanged glances. Truman cleared his throat before addressing Pastor Schaefer.

"Sir, I guess you might say I have a professional question to ask of you."

Pastor Schaefer waited with a puzzled expression for Truman to continue.

"Sallie and I would like to marry, and we would like for you to do the honors."

"Oh!" gasped Marta, and she moved to give Sallie a hug.

Little Jeremy nudged his sister and said. "I knew he liked her—I just knew it!"

"Of course I will marry the two of you. Nothing could make me happier!" Pastor Schaefer replied with heartfelt sincerity.

The next day, the families of the wagon train took notice of the change in the general lay of the land. The roll of the prairie had given way to a trail that definitely was more uphill than down. As a result of the steeper grade, the livestock needed more frequent stops to rest. The late afternoon sun found the drivers circling the wagons for the evening near a picturesque, tree-lined stream surrounded by low hills.

Word had quickly spread among the families that day as to the wedding to be held in the evening at Pastor Schaefer's wagon for Sallie Brewster and Truman Garrett. The wagons had stopped a little earlier in the day than usual, and the women had taken advantage of the additional daylight to prepare some special foods. It was surprising, considering the rough conditions of living outdoors, but with the collective creative talents of a number of the ladies, a wedding meal was soon taking shape.

Dale Carter could be heard tuning his fiddle and playing a sweet-sounding melody. He had been pleased when Sallie Brewster had asked if he would play.

Little Meg could be seen picking and arranging some colorful flowers for a bouquet for the bride-to-be.

Grinder was down at the stream, taking special care to trim his mustache and then select his best shirt from his saddlebag. He had been asked by Truman to be his best man. Grinder had never been asked to serve in this capacity before and was taking this request very seriously. He could be heard questioning Jake Willard about duties he would be expected to perform.

Marta was going to be her friend's matron of honor. She helped Sallie choose between a green dress and a blue gingham one. The blue was chosen. Then Marta helped Meg arrange the flowers she had picked and tied them together with a pretty bow of blue ribbon.

Truman had a white cloth shirt, which he seldom wore, packed at the bottom of his saddlebag. He pulled it out and shook the wrinkles out the best he could. Holding it up to examine it, he realized it definitely needed the touch of an iron, but it would have to do.

Sallie had slipped into the blue dress and brushed through her long tresses. As she twisted and secured the hair to form a bun at the back of her head, just slightly above her dress collar, she paused, pondering the events of the past few months. A couple of months prior, she would have laughed if anyone had suggested she might marry again, let alone before reaching her destination.

"Sallie? Can I be of help?" Marta called to her, interrupting her reverie.

"I think I'm ready," answered Sallie.

Sallie climbed down from the wagon. Seeing Meg standing beside her mother holding the ribbon wrapped flowers, she exclaimed. "Oh, Meg, the flowers are beautiful!"

The three walked toward the Schaefer's wagon, where a number of people had already gathered. Pastor Schaefer was standing, his Bible open to the scripture he planned to read. Jeremy was beside him with an almost angelic smile on his little round, cherubic face.

Truman and Grinder arrived. Sallie noted how handsome Truman was. She couldn't recall having seen him dressed in anything other than his buckskin clothing before.

Pastor Schaefer directed the wedding party to their positions. Then he began the service. The rest of the wedding quickly moved forward, and when Pastor Schaefer pronounced Truman and Sallie to be man and wife, a collective shout erupted from the assembled crowd. Dale Carter began to play a lovely, gentle melody on his fiddle. The newlyweds were congratulated and then people began to drift toward the tables laden with food. They waited for the pastor to bless the food and then began to fill their plates. When the meal was nearly over, Dale Carter began to play again, and this time picked up the tempo with a rollicking tune. Soon, a festive feeling was definitely in the air. It was difficult to sit still listening to the lively melodies, and soon here and there people were starting to dance. As twilight approached, lanterns were lit, and a couple of campfires were kept going into the evening. The party continued well into the evening. A sleepy Jeremy was carried off to bed by his dad.

17

Too soon, the first rays of light began to color the eastern sky. It was time to gather the stock and prepare for another day of travel. If all went as planned today and the wagons made good time traveling, Mr. McMasters indicated that by tomorrow, the wagons should be at the fork in the trail, where a number of the families planned to leave the train. The Schaefers would be one of those families. Not too far from that fork in the trail existed a small but growing settlement of families of mostly German background. They had come to worship and live in freedom. These were the people who had written to Pastor Schaefer, asking him to come to their valley. They were building a church and needed him to be their pastor.

Sallie and Truman would also be leaving the wagon train at this point. Sallie's son's home was not far beyond the valley where their friends, the Schaefers, would be making a new life.

That day, the road continued steadily upward, which required resting the stock frequently. By midafternoon, it was a relief when they reached a high, fairly level plateau. The road continued along this plateau for the rest of the day.

As the wagons pulled into a circle that evening, some of them for the last time, there seemed to be a special mood of anticipation about the group. The realization that the end of the trail was near and they would soon be starting a new life in a new land was on everyone's minds. Even for those whose wagons would be continuing on somewhat farther, it would only be about a week or so of more travel.

This was an especially poignant evening in the camp for many of the families, as some of them would be parting tomorrow, never to meet again. Friendships had been formed during the many miles of travel. They had relied on each other many times for survival through the hardships on the many miles of trail. The travelers had shared laughter and tears. In many ways, they had become stronger individuals from skills they had learned from each other. There was much visiting between the wagons that evening, with promises made to try to somehow keep in touch. However, most knew in their hearts they would never hear from some of their friends again.

As the sun rose in a cloudless sky the next morning, the travelers were already up preparing for the day. Mr. McMasters and Truman Garrett shook hands for the last time.

"Ma'am," McMasters said to Sallie, "I'll admit I sure had my worries about letting a lone woman continue on with the wagons, but you proved yourself capable and resourceful enough to make it. I send my best wishes for success with you and Truman as you make a life together. From what I have observed, if any two people are prepared to make it out here, the two of you certainly will." With that comment, the wagon master placed his old brown hat on his head and turned back to the task of preparing the remaining people for the day's travel.

Grinder and Harry also bid farewell to the departing families. The two men would be continuing with the train. They were fully capable of handling the needs of the people for the rest of the trip.

"We'll be sure to look in on y'all from time to time when we come back by here," promised Grinder as he pumped Truman's hand. "Me and Henry will be sure to get a cravin' for Mrs. Brewster's—I mean Mrs. Garrett's—biscuits, and y'all will find a couple of old scouts on your doorstep." With that, he tipped his hat and smiled in Sallie's direction.

"I hope you both will do that," Sallie replied.

Harry cleared his throat, and, removing his hat, almost bashfully spoke to the now Mrs. Garrett. "Ma'am, I can't say how much we appreciate all the times you and Mrs. Schaefer cooked for us. I confess I been really payin' attention as to how y'all made those biscuits and such, but just don't think I can manage to turn out somethin' as tasty as the two of y'all. Grinder and I will just have to go back to fendin' for ourselves soon."

It was hard seeing the two old friends walk away to take their places helping the people continuing westward.

Looking up at Truman standing next to her, Sallie whispered, "I do hope they will come."

Truman smiled. "Oh, I have a feeling we haven't seen the last of those two."

This time, Sallie's wagon was in the lead, and Truman was riding in front of the little group. The Schaefers' wagon rolled directly behind them, followed by the rest of the wagons as they took the northward fork in the trail. With the rolling terrain, plus the addition of trees at the higher elevation, all too soon the other wagon train disappeared from sight.

Even with a couple of stops to rest the animals on the now steeper and narrower trail, by early afternoon the wagons crested the top of a long grade to view a valley below with the small settlement that was to be the future home to most of them. The church that was waiting for Pastor Schaefer could be seen far down below. The pastor, sitting next to Marta in the wagon, put his arm around his wife and pointed.

"There it is. Just like they described it in the letters. We're almost home."

The children peeked excitedly around either side of their parents.

In unison, Meg and Jeremy exclaimed, "Look! Look!"

The trail made a gradual descent. Often, the valley was hidden from view by trees or boulders. Finally, after one last curve, the trail leveled out and followed a wide stream flowing in the direction of the town. The water sparkled in the afternoon sun. A doe on the far bank, interrupted while quenching her thirst, raised her head to stare for a moment at the leading wagon before gracefully turning and disappearing into the brush behind her. As the valley became wider, smaller trails appeared, leading off into the trees. Sometimes a house could be seen through the trees, and at other times the trails just led off mysteriously into the wilderness. However, fresh wheel ruts and hoof prints in the road gave evidence that the wagons were nearing civilization.

As the travelers continued onward, the side lanes appeared more frequently, and homes were built closer to the road. People could now be seen pausing in the fields or stepping out on porches to stare at the approaching wagons. A couple of men were seen riding toward the wagons. They reined their horses to a halt to one side of the road and waited as the wagons approached. Sallie was driving the lead wagon with Truman riding the grulla mustang alongside the lead mules. The townsmen sat patiently for Truman to ride closer before attempting conversation.

"Hello! Could this be the group traveling with Pastor Schaefer?" the older of the two men inquired.

Truman nodded and, turning in his saddle, he pointed to the wagon directly behind Sallie's. "Yes, he is right here."

As Pastor Schaefer pulled his mules to a halt, the middle-aged rider, seeing the pastor's clerical collar, greeted, "Hello, I'm Karl Obendorf. You must be Pastor Schaefer."

There was a slight hint of an accent in his deep baritone voice.

"Yes, I am, and this is my wife, Marta. Could you be the Karl Obendorf that wrote the letter requesting a pastor for your church?"

"Ja, I am the one," he replied as he nudged his horse forward so that he could shake the pastor's hand in welcome. The other man came forward and introduced himself, also leaning forward on his horse to shake the Pastor's hand.

"I am Peter Richter. We have been looking forward to your arrival. The church has been built, and we have even completed a house nearby. We hope that you will be pleased."

"Peter is very skilled," said Karl. "He was the one who designed the church. It is very pretty. But, you have traveled far and must be very tired. Come, follow us."

The two men turned their mounts and led the way into town.

The little settlement was very neat and tidy, almost like a little jewel surrounded by the mountains on seemingly all sides. All of the buildings appeared to be fairly new. Most of the wagons stopped just outside of town in a level grassy area where Karl Obendorf indicated they would have plenty of water and enough shade for a pleasant evening camp. Then, in the morning, the travelers could look the area over to decide what their next steps would be. There was a definite air of excitement about the wagons. They were finally home. This was their promised land. Their hardships of the trail were over. Now the new challenge of establishing a home in the wilderness was at hand.

Pastor Schaefer paused the mules long enough to watch as the wagons began to pull off the trail into the lovely open meadow. Then he motioned to Truman, who was now astride the grulla, to come alongside the wagon. Truman guided his horse over to hear what the pastor had to say.

"Truman, why don't you and Sallie follow us on into town tonight? We can look over the house and church together. Then, if you want to get started toward Sallie's son's place tomorrow, you can, or if you just want to rest a few days here with us, that's okay too."

Truman nodded, reined his horse around, and headed back toward Sallie's wagon to share the plan with her.

"Of course! That sounds great," Sallie agreed upon hearing the suggestion.

The two wagons continued through town to the little house and lovely little church. Upon closer view, they saw that someone had carved some lovely decorative woodwork on the porch surrounding the front of the church, which was repeated on the porch of the house next door—the Schaefers' new home.

"Oh, I never expected they would build a house for us, and such a lovely one!" Marta exclaimed.

The wagons were stopped side by side. The men unhitched the teams and turned them into a little paddock area. Once the mule teams and horses were given food and water, the group proceeded toward the house. Karl Obendorf and Peter Richter were obviously anxious for the pastor to see what the people had worked so hard to have ready in time for their new pastor. After leading the way to the house, Karl stepped to one side of the front door and Peter to the other side. Both men bowed slightly and with a sweep of one arm indicated that the Schaefers were to enter first. Marta stepped across the threshold first and then stopped.

She softly exclaimed, "Oh, it even has a board floor!" She then proceeded with a rapt expression on her face to investigate the several rooms. At the rear of the house was a ladder leading to a loft area.

Marta turned to her husband, giving him a wide-eyed look of wonderment. "Never did I expect this."

The pastor just stood with a pleased smile on his face, his look of wonderment almost matching that of his wife.

The children were following close behind, hand in hand.

"Who lives here?" Jeremy whispered to his sister.

"We will. This is our new home," answered their father.

"Wow!" the children whispered in unison.

Returning to the front room, where Mr. Obendorf and Mr. Richter were waiting with Truman and Sallie, the pastor reached out his hand and pumped those of the two men who had been instrumental in bringing the Schaefers to this little town in the mountains.

"Words can't express how grateful we are for all of this. We never expected a house too. Thank you so much!"

Marta stood beside him and just nodded. She wasn't able to speak, as tears of gratitude were threatening to spill from her eyes.

"You are so welcome. We all felt you should not have the burden of building a house, but should be free to establish our church and meet the needs of the congregation," explained Mr. Richter with a smile.

"Oh, Sallie, come see." Marta had finally managed to find her voice, and reaching for Sallie's hand, led her through the other rooms of the house so her friend could see for herself how blessed the Schaefers were.

The men started out the door in the direction of the church. Soon the women followed, with the wide-eyed children, still hand in hand, following behind.

The little church proved to have been built with the same expertise and care as the house. There were even pews instead of benches in place. They all paused for a moment just inside the door to take it all in.

Then Mr. Obendorf spoke. "The Lord has blessed our congregation with many dedicated and skilled men and women."

The pastor strode to the front of the church. A wooden cross hung on the wall overlooking the simple wooden altar. Kneeling before the altar, he bowed his head and offered a silent prayer of thanks to the Lord for His protection during the westward journey and guidance for the future. Upon rising, he stepped to the wooden pulpit and turned to look out over the room.

"Lord, please give me the words of wisdom to bring your message to these people," he offered in a whisper.

Pastor Schaefer then stepped down from the pulpit and turned and bowed toward the altar before proceeding toward the rear of church where the two elders and his family and friends waited.

As the little group walked the short distance back to the Schaefer's new home, Karl Obendorf and Peter Richter introduced the Schaefer family to some of the members of the congregation who had gathered to meet the pastor.

Upon returning to the house, it was discovered that a covered-dish supper had been organized to welcome the Schaefers. Food was arranged on tables and some quilts spread on the ground. After the blessing was given, the conversation again resumed. Everyone was anxious to meet the new pastor and his wife. Upon filling their plates, the younger members seated themselves on the quilts, leaving the few chairs for the older people. Marta motioned for Sallie and Truman to sit by them.

As Marta was engaged in conversation with one of the ladies, Sallie was thinking with a touch of sadness that this would be their last evening together for quite some time. In the morning, Truman would be hitching up the team for the last day of travel. Just the two of them would be continuing on from this little town. They would only be about a day's travel away, but how often they might be able to visit was something she didn't want to let her mind dwell on right now. After being so much a part of these special people's lives for so many months, it was painful to dwell on the realization she and Truman would be leaving them behind in the morning.

Sallie was vaguely aware of the conversation Truman and a middle-aged man who was dressed more like a rancher than a farmer were having. However, she noted that Truman seemed to startle slightly when the man mentioned the name Delbert Harley.

"You say Del Harley has a cattle operation in this area?"

"Yes, you know him?"

"The name seems familiar" was the only comment Truman made.

"There is excellent pastureland northwest of here—actually, in the direction you will be traveling. Harley has quite a successful spread out there."

The man continued describing the merits of the grassland they would see after they climbed out of the valley the next day to head toward Sallie's son's place. However, Truman was now lost in his own thoughts and absorbed little of the ensuing conversation.

He was thinking about his past rearing its evil head. He had not told Sallie about Harley. Oh, how could he have been such a fool to think that he could leave his past behind and lead a normal life? What would she think of the mistake he had made so long ago? If she knew he had served time, would she still stand by him? Would she want to introduce him to her son and his family?

Then he felt the old, long-buried anger rising to the surface. Harley had used him. Truman excused himself and strode away from the crowd. He needed to regain his composure and to think. Reaching the fence enclosing the mules and horses behind the little house, he paused, resting his elbows on the top rail. He gazed out at the mountains, seeing not the rocky ridges, but his own past. The grulla nickered a greeting, walked over, and nuzzled Truman's shoulder. Truman reached out to the horse and began stroking his neck.

"I don't belong with these good church folks—not with this hate in my heart. Pastor Schaefer would tell me to forgive Harley. How can I forgive a man like that?" Truman said, resting his hand on the horse's neck. The mustang remained still, almost as if he was listening and understood the human's pain.

Truman made his decision. Walking to the rear of Sallie's wagon, he pulled his Sharps out of its scabbard. Then, finding what he needed in his saddlebag, he sat down on a log and began to clean his rifle. After also checking over his pistol, he put everything away. He pulled the grulla out of the pasture, saddled him, and attached the scabbard containing the rifle. Then Truman strode around the corner of the cabin. Seeing Pastor Schaefer talking to a couple of men near the porch of the house, he managed to catch the man's attention and indicated that he needed to have a word with him.

When the pastor approached, Truman explained, "I have some business to attend to. Can Sallie stay with you and Marta for a few days?"

"Of course. Is something wrong?" asked the concerned pastor, noting the stern expression on Truman's face.

"I have some business to attend to," he repeated.

Sallie noticed the pastor and Truman talking. Then Truman started in her direction. He led her a little apart from the assembled people before beginning.

"Sallie, there is something I have to take care of, and I need to leave you here for a few days with the Schaefers."

"Truman, what is it? I thought we would be leaving in the morning for Jim's place." She felt a knot of concern begin to form in her stomach. When she started to speak again, a kiss silenced her.

He started to walk away. She followed him around the corner of the house, and then, seeing his horse saddled and ready to go, she stopped.

"Truman, where are you going?"

After quickly mounting, he leaned down from his horse and gently brushed a stray strand of hair from her face. Their eyes met. He seemed to be looking deep into her soul. Would he see her again? Then he turned his horse and was gone.

Sallie stood, shaken by his departure. Fear choked her. She felt she couldn't move. What was happening?

She stood for a long time in shock. Then Sallie tried to search her memory for a hint of something someone had said or done that could have caused him to ride off like this. She walked over to her wagon, and when she looked inside, she saw that it appeared he had taken most of his belongings. His extra horse was still in the pasture.

The sun was behind the mountains now. Sallie reached behind the seat in the front of the wagon to fetch her shawl as the rapidly approaching twilight brought a chill in the air. As she turned from the wagon and wrapped the shawl around her shoulders, Sallie again stared in disbelief in the direction Truman had gone.

"Sallie!" Marta was calling her. "There you are. Hans told me Truman rode off to take care of some kind of business and would be gone for a few days. Let me help you get what you need out of the wagon and come inside."

Sallie now realized all the people had gone home. It was just the Schaefers and her now.

As the ladies entered the back door, the pastor was coming down the ladder from the loft, having just tucked the children in for the night.

Not having much in the way of furniture, the ladies sat down on the large raised hearth in the front room. The pastor brought in a few logs from out back and soon had a fire going that cast flickering fingers of light on the bare walls of the room.

"Are you all right, Sallie?" inquired Marta, her tone worried. "Did Truman say where he was going?"

Sallie just shook her head. Then, finally finding her voice, she softly said, "All he would say was that he needed to leave me here for a few days and take care of something. I've been trying to rethink everything that happened today for some idea of what might be wrong."

"Sallie, maybe he just wants to surprise you with something. Why do you think something is wrong?"

"The way he looked at me before he rode off, like … like … It was almost like he wasn't sure he would see me again. I don't know. I have been trying to remember if something was said. The only thing I can recall overhearing was part of a conversation he was having with a man. He was telling Truman something about a man who had a successful cattle operation near here. I remember that when he mentioned the man's name—Del or Delbert Hartly, or maybe it was Harley—Truman seemed startled, and shortly afterward he disappeared around the back of the house.

"Oh, Pastor, do you think this could be someone from his past? He had warned me about something like that."

"I'll ask around in the morning. See what I can find out." Then, bowing his head and folding his hands, he said "But first let us pray for Truman. God grant Truman the wisdom to use good judgment. Keep him safe in body, mind, and spirit and bring Truman back to us soon, free from whatever might be troubling him. In the dear name of Jesus, we pray. Amen."

Then, turning to Sallie, he said, "We have put Truman in God's hands now, Sallie. Trust Him."

Sallie nodded. She felt comforted. The panic and choking fear she had felt earlier had subsided. Just an overwhelming tiredness seemed to engulf her now.

"Spread your blankets by the fire tonight. There is a bit of a chill in the night air here," instructed Marta, a concerned expression on her face.

Marta and the pastor retired to their room in the rear of the house. By then, Sallie was asleep. She slept fitfully that night, waking to lie thinking and worrying about Truman. When she felt the panic returning, she would whisper, "Trust. Trust."

18

Truman rode until he could no longer make out the trail in the darkness ahead. After dismounting and leading the mustang a short distance from the trail, he lifted the saddle and lay down on his blankets. Sleep did not come immediately. Memories kept surfacing in his tortured mind. What would he do if this was the Del Harley from his past? What would Del Harley's reaction be to seeing Truman Garrett after all of these years? Could he—or should he—return to Sallie? Maybe he wouldn't even be able to return to her. She had come to mean so very much to him.

With a start he opened his eyes and sat up. The faint first light of dawn was beginning to filter through the leaves of the tree above his head. His mustang stood nearby, ears alert, watching a small animal moving down the slope toward a little stream. Perhaps it was a beaver. It was hard to be sure in the dim light. Only the top of its furry back was visible as it pushed its way through the undergrowth.

With a grunt, Truman rose to his feet, rubbing his back where a tree's root had made its impression. Soon he had gathered his gear and had the grulla ready to travel.

By late morning, he came to a crossroads of sorts. A small general store stood near the junction. It appeared that the store occupied one side of the building, and on the other side was a room that might pass for a saloon. Truman stopped long enough to purchase some beef jerky from its cheerful proprietor and ask directions to the Harley place. He managed to avoid answering the man's questions about how he came to be in this part of the country.

The directions proved to be accurate. By afternoon, he spotted the ranch house in the distance. The rancher at the pastor's house had certainly been correct in his praise of the good grassland in this part of the country. He could see many fat cattle grazing as he approached. Reining his horse to a halt under a large tree on top of a rise of ground, he mulled over how he should approach. Should he scout the place out or just ride in? He decided on the latter after viewing the spread. He didn't see much adult activity. A couple of children were playing near the house with a puppy. They appeared to be about ten or twelve years of age. As he rode up to the house, a sweet-faced woman stepped out on the porch of what was a rather large log home.

"Hello, ma'am. Is Del at home?" he politely inquired.

"My husband's over at the barn. I don't recall making your acquaintance before. You look like you've traveled far. Help yourself to some water there at the well. Just pull up on that rope. There is a bucket tied to it," she offered kindly.

"Thank you, ma'am." He touched his hat in respect and turned his horse in the direction of the barn.

After dismounting, he dropped the end of one of his reins to the ground to let the well-trained horse know to stand. The other rein was left over the horse's neck in case he should need to remount and leave in a hurry. Cautiously, Truman entered the barn and stepped to one side of the doorway so as not to be standing exposed in the middle of the opening as his eyes adjusted to the dimmer light. Hearing movement in a rear stall of the building, he carefully approached the sound. In one of the stalls, a stocky, balding, middle-aged man was bent over, applying some medication to a cut on a horse's leg.

The man straightened and patted the horse's shoulder. He then turned and saw Truman standing there. First an expression of surprise appeared on his face. Then the color seemed to drain as he recognized Truman Garrett. He just stood there, dumbfounded, with the open can of salve in one hand and the other hand still resting on the horse.

"Garrett ... Truman Garrett," he finally managed to say. "Please. I don't want any trouble. I know you have every right to hate me for what I did to you. I did you wrong. I was a coward for running out and leaving you like that. I'll give you anything you want if you just won't tell Mary and the children what I was. Mary and I have built this spread by honest means. It may be hard for you to believe, but not one head of these cattle was stolen. This may sound strange to you too, but by the grace of God and a good woman's love, I've changed from a cattle thief into an honest man. Please. I mean it. I'll give you anything you want if you will just ride away and not say anything to them."

"Harley, there isn't anything you can give me to replace the time I spent in jail or the time spent clearing my name afterward. I trusted you and you took advantage of me. You wanted a hired gun, not a cowhand. I was never a gun for hire. I can understand a good woman's influence. I'll admit I came here to even a score, but—somehow it's over. I'll be leaving now, and I hope we never meet again."

Truman turned and strode out to his waiting horse. He stepped into the stirrup, mounted, and without further comment turned his horse and rode down the trail to the main road and out of Harley's life forever.

Harley stood in the barn doorway, still holding the can of salve, watching as Truman rode away. "He could have easily killed me if he'd wanted," Harley had developed a habit of talking aloud to himself over the years. "I wouldn't have had a chance even if I'd had a gun. Garrett was the best. I've lived in fear of him riding in like this, and now it's happened. He's leaving, and I'm still alive." As he approached the house, he realized Mary was standing on the porch watching the rider depart as he had just done.

"Was he an old friend? Why didn't you invite him to supper?" she inquired.

"Oh, he was someone I knew a long time ago, and he had to be on his way."

Truman rode along, lost in thought. He marveled that somehow he felt lighter. When he reached the main road, he reined the mustang to a stop. Turning in his saddle, he looked back up the lane toward the house. For years, he had carried revenge in his heart when he thought of that man. Somehow the man seemed so different now. Truman remembered Harley's words—"by the grace of God and a good woman's love." Truman and the grulla stood there a moment longer. Then, with a shake of his head, Truman made his decision and turned the mustang back toward the little village in the mountain valley. He was going back to Sallie. If a man like Harley could change, maybe he could too. Maybe he already had. As he passed by the little isolated store again, the proprietor standing in the doorway waved. Garret returned the greeting but continued on until darkness once again made the mountain road too difficult to travel. He and the mustang found a little cove to spend the night. This time Garrett's sleep was less troubled.

—⊨⊨—

The morning after Truman left, Pastor Schaefer asked around town to see if anyone knew a man named Hartly or Harley. All he was able to learn was that a man by the name of Harley was said to have arrived in this part of the county fifteen to twenty years ago. He had settled in another valley northwest of the village and had built a successful cattle operation. None of the individuals the pastor questioned had actually met the man.

Sallie had spent the time after Truman left helping Marta unload the Schaefers' wagon and put away the few belongings they had brought with them. Frequently, she would pause to check the road in the direction Truman had ridden, hoping to see him returning. She tried not to dwell on the memory of the stern expression on his face and the feeling that something from his past was pulling him away from her.

It had been two days and two nights since Truman had ridden out. Sallie, Marta, and Meg were preparing the evening meal, and little Jeremy had followed his father over to the church.

"Olga Meier said she would trade one of her hens for a couple of jars of my strawberry jam," said Marta. "I thought Meg and I could walk out to her place tomorrow. Do you want to come with us, Sallie?"

Marta's hands were covered in flour as she kneaded some dough for biscuits for the evening meal.

Sallie hesitated a moment, thinking that that would mean she would not be at the house if Truman returned.

"I ... I don't know. Perhaps—" she began to answer. Then, hearing a sound, she turned.

Truman stood in the doorway. With a little gasp, she set down the pitcher she was holding and rushed to him.

"Oh, Truman, I was so worried."

Marta motioned to Meg to follow her into the other room in order to give her friends some privacy.

"Sallie, I hope you can forgive me for leaving like that. There was, well, just something I had to work out."

Sallie stepped back and looked up into his eyes, searching for an answer. Finally, she asked, "Well, did you ... work it out?"

Truman nodded. How could he explain? The bitterness and anger that had for so many years burned in his mind whenever thoughts of Harley crossed his mind was gone. A weight was lifted.

Jeremy's excited voice could be heard from the other room. "Meg, come look! Puppy!"

The pastor's voice could be heard explaining, "George Miller stopped by as we were leaving the church. He asked if we would like a pup for the children."

Truman and Sallie joined the pastor and Marta on the porch. Jeremy and Meg were sitting on the ground with a little brown and white puppy darting back and forth between them. The pup appeared as excited to have them in his world as they were to have him. His whole body wagged along with his long tail.

The pastor and Truman walked around the back of the house. Truman took care of his horse as the two men talked.

After the men walked around back, Marta turned to Sallie. "Did he say where he went?"

"No, he just nodded when I asked if he had been able to work out whatever it was. He seemed reluctant to talk. Maybe he will tell me about it later. You know, I was actually afraid he wouldn't come back."

Sallie and Marta entered the house to finish supper preparations. The children were oblivious to the adults' departure. They were totally distracted with the antics of the playful puppy.

Due to the lack of furniture, the adults ate their meal sitting on crates and barrels they had unloaded from the wagon. The children sat cross-legged on the floor of the kitchen. The pastor had assured Marta that morning that one of his first projects would be to build a table.

19

After breakfast, Sallie and Truman loaded the few items they had needed for their stay with the Schaefers back onto the wagon. Truman hitched the mules and tied the three horses to the back of the wagon. It didn't take long to have everything ready for travel.

After hugs and handshakes, the friends parted with promises for future visits whenever they could. Truman and Sallie traveled in silence for the first few miles. Each was lost in his or her own thoughts.

The road continued beside the stream until, nearing the end of the valley, it took a turn to the left and began to wind its way upward. After they reached the top of the rather steep grade, Truman halted the mules so they could rest. Looking back, all they could see above the trees in the valley was the steeple of the little church.

Truman started the team forward once again, and the only sounds to be heard were the jingling of the harness, the creaking of the wagon, and the rhythmic beat of hooves on the trail.

"Sallie, I owe you an explanation for riding off like that. There was a man many years ago that hired me to work cattle on his place. At least that was what I thought in the beginning. I hired on as a simple cowhand, and I was thankful to find the work. Guess I was kind of naïve. Even after some things just didn't add up with the daily operation, it took me awhile to become suspicious that this guy, Harley, was not what he seemed to be. On the one hand, he seemed to be a likable, easygoing kind of guy. But as I got to know him, I found that he had a habit of telling half-truths or twisting the truth to suit his own needs."

"One day he confided that a certain gunman might come looking for him. This gunman was said to hold a grudge over some girl they had both been in love with. Harley said they had fought over her. He told me the other man drew his gun to shoot Harley, but the girl tried to grab the gun. In the struggle, the gun went off, and she was killed. The man was said to have vowed he would hunt Harley down and kill him."

"It was just a couple of days after he shared this story with me that a stranger appeared in town. Talk reached us out on the ranch that a stranger who called himself Buford Buckner was in town asking around if anyone knew of a man named Delbert Harley. He claimed to be looking for an old friend."

"Right away, Harley said to me, 'True, you've got to help me. I'm no match for Buckner with a gun. With fists, I can better the man easily. But I'm no good with a gun. It won't be a fistfight this time. This guy will be gunning for me for sure. I need your help.'"

"I told him I didn't want to be involved in any trouble, but would see what I could do."

"Then things happened so quickly, it's still hard to sort it all out. I remember Harley saying something about needing to check on a mare before dark that was about ready to foal. As he was saddling his horse to ride out to check on the mare, three strangers appeared on the lane to the house. The next thing I heard was the sound of Harley's horse leaving at a run out the back of the barn."

"The three strangers spread out and rode on in with guns drawn. I saw right away they were wearing badges on their vests and, with hands up, let them know I didn't want any trouble. Then one of the men identified himself as Buford Buckner (turned out he was really the law) and I was told I was under arrest for being involved with an illegal cattle operation."

"Delbert Harley made his getaway while all this was happening. He set me up. Harley must have known those men were on the way out to the ranch that afternoon. While they were busy arresting me, he just slipped away and disappeared. The law never caught up with him. At first, they even thought I was Harley! They assumed I was the one running the operation. It turned out those little trips to "buy cattle" that Harley took from time to time were really excursions to rustle a few head from some ranches on the other side of the range. He would only take a few head here and there (no more than one man could handle) and drive them into a backcountry canyon until he could doctor the brand, or, if they were unbranded, he'd just go ahead and put one on. This way he was able to get away undetected for quite a while on his own. Then he decided he needed to get a hired gun for protection when some suspicion began to arise as to the honesty of his operation."

"Well, I went to jail, and it was a couple of years before I was able to get out and start over. I was determined to hunt him down and get even with him for what he had done to me. Harley seemed to have just totally disappeared. The trail was cold. No matter how hard I tried, I couldn't track him down. He just seemed to have vanished from the face of the earth."

"Guess I had given up ever finding him. Whenever I'd think of him, anger would kind of gnaw at me. Finally, after years of finding no trace of him, I figured he must be dead. Hearing his name several nights ago brought everything back. I had to find out. Had to know if it was him. I rode out not knowing what I would find or what I would do if it were him."

"Sallie, he was a changed man—or maybe it's me that has changed. He'd aged and had a family. He even offered me whatever I wanted if I just wouldn't tell his family what he had been. Anyway, the anger and the bitterness that I had always felt when thinking of Harley had somehow left me, and I just rode away. It's hard to explain, but I finally feel free from that part of my past."

"Oh, Truman, I'm glad you told me. I—I didn't know what was wrong and was so worried when you rode out like that." Sallie slid her arm around his waist.

They were resting their team about midday when three young men rode up. There was something about the way they sat upon their horses that put Truman on the alert. He had just saddled the grulla and was planning on riding a little ahead of the mules after the noon rest. The approaching strangers rode with reins held in their left hands, and their other hands were resting on the handles of their holstered guns.

Sallie had climbed back onto the wagon seat and taken the lines into her hands in readiness for what they hoped would be the last leg of the trip. She didn't notice the approaching riders until they were almost upon the wagon. Even then, she didn't feel alarmed at the three men riding their horses toward them on the road.

The men stopped in front of Truman, and Sallie could hear one of them address Truman in a nasty tone of voice. "Old man, I really admire that Sharps you got in your scabbard. Think you should just hand it over to me."

As the rider spoke, with almost lightning speed, he drew his gun. Suddenly, there was a loud blast as three guns were drawn and fired. Sallie screamed. A startled expression appeared on the man's face who had demanded Truman's Sharps, and then he fell from his horse. The frightened animal bolted as the man fell. Another one of the men also fell from his horse. The second man hit the ground with a groan and rolled over onto his stomach.

The third rider, who hadn't drawn his weapon, threw up his hands, screaming, "Don't shoot! Don't shoot!"

A faint wisp of smoke could be seen drifting from Truman's gun as it was pointed at the third man.

Truman kicked the guns away from the two fallen men. "Unbuckle your gun belt with one hand and throw it on the ground," he ordered the man still mounted.

When the man had complied, Truman commanded, "Keep your hands over your head!"

Truman confirmed that the first rider was dead and that the second man didn't have a concealed weapon on him. He then ordered the third man to dismount.

"I ain't going to give you any trouble."

"Load him on one of your horses." Truman indicated the motionless man.

After he was lifted and laid across the saddle of one of the two remaining horses, the injured man slowly staggered to his feet with his left hand clutching his bleeding upper right arm. The third man tied his bandanna tightly just above the wound in an attempt to stop the blood flow and helped his companion onto his horse. With that done, he climbed on behind the somewhat dazed man. In his left hand, he held the reins of his horse, and in his right hand Truman placed the reins of the horse carrying the dead man. Urging his horse forward, he started off without a backward glance. Awkwardly, the men slowly departed in the direction they had come with one horse carrying two men and the second horse with a single load across the saddle.

Truman watched until the riders disappeared down a right fork in the trail before holstering his gun. He turned and for the first time realized Sallie was on the wagon seat with her shotgun out and ready for backup.

"I reckon you can put that away now. I don't think those young toughs will be bothering anybody for a while."

"Truman, are you okay?"

Truman nodded and walked over to retrieve the reins of his horse. The mustang had moved off a short distance during all of the commotion. He picked up his reins, stepped into the stirrup, and mounted, all the while keeping his eyes on the road ahead.

"We'd best be moving on down the road," Truman called out to her and motioned toward the left fork in the trail.

Sallie urged the mules forward, and soon the wagon was once again moving westward. However, Sallie's heart was beating faster, and she was nervously scanning the hilltops and trees along the trail for further danger that might be lurking. She found herself startling at movement near the trail only to have it turn out to be a deer.

Truman and Sallie continued on in silence. Truman, ever watchful, was deep in thought. He knew he had done what he had to do in order to keep himself and Sallie safe, but it deeply disturbed him to have taken a life. A man had to be able to protect himself and his own in this beautiful but lawless land. He wondered if there would indeed come a time when it would be different and if he would live to see that day. A weariness seemed to settle around him.

It had been a couple of hours since the incident at the fork in the road. Truman had hoped they would make it to Sallie's son's place by sundown, but with the time lost, it seemed best to stop someplace and continue on in the morning. A small clearing appeared near the trail. There would be enough grass for the livestock to be content for the night. Truman indicated to Sallie to pull off the trail. After tending to the animals' needs, they pulled the few items they would need for the evening's meal from the wagon. Few words were spoken as they picked up some dry branches to build a fire. Sallie could tell Truman was troubled. It wasn't until Truman was kneeling to place an additional branch on the fire he was building that she noticed the tear in the shoulder of his buckskin shirt and the reddened skin showing through it where a bullet had burned his shoulder.

Tears sprang to her eyes as she reached out to Truman and whispered. "Oh, Truman, you are hurt!"

He seemed not to have noticed until she spoke. Then, glancing at his shoulder, he just said, "It's nothing." He continued to build the fire.

Truman remained somewhat withdrawn during the simple preparations for the meal. They ate without conversation. Sallie finally broke the silence.

"Truman, do you think those men will be coming after us?"

"Doubt it."

"You're so quiet."

"Sallie, thought it was past me."

When she looked puzzled as to his meaning, Truman pulled his pistol out of his holster. He looked down at it and turned it from side to side, studying it as if seeing it for the first time.

"I took a life this afternoon. How can you live with a man capable of that? Yes, if I hadn't, one or both of us would now be dead. But … what would the preacher say?"

"Oh, Truman, you stopped him! You stopped all of them. They would have killed us. God understands. The Bible talks about there being a time for everything. It says there is a time to fight and a time for peace," she said. "I love you."

Sallie went to him, wrapping her arms around him. They remained seated by the fire until the flames had died to just a golden glow.

About the time Truman and Sallie were pulling off the trail for the night, two of the men who had attempted to rob them were finally making it back to the log cabin they called home. A middle-aged man stepped out the door to meet them as they rode up, leading the horse carrying the dead man.

"Looks like you boys ran into some difficulty," the older man observed dryly.

"I'd say so," answered the only man in shape for conversation.

"Help me get Clayton down and into the cabin. I think he's about all done in."

The two men helped the one called Clayton from the horse and into the cabin. He was guided toward a cot in the corner of the one-room cabin. Then the older man turned toward the door to head back out to the horses.

"You tend to Clayton. I'll get Wes down and unsaddle the horses. We can bury Wes in the morning. Reckon there's no hurry. Figured you boys had run into trouble when Wes's horse came back this afternoon with blood on the saddle."

The younger man carried a pan out to the mountain stream near the cabin, and, after filling it with cold fresh water, went back inside to care for the injured man's wound. After cleaning and wrapping the wound, he found Clayton's spare shirt and helped him get it on. Clayton nodded his thanks, slowly lay back down on the cot with a groan, and closed his eyes.

The older man, having finished taking care of the livestock, appeared at the cabin door. Pausing, he indicated the man on the cot.

"How's he doing?"

"Clayton's lost a lot of blood, but he's resting now."

"Tell me what happened."

"Well, we were going to ride over to Conyers. Then we saw this settler's wagon stopped along the road. There was just a man and a woman as far as we could see. Wes figured we could just ride up to them, show our guns, and take what we wanted. He said it would be easy.

"I remember Clayton had hesitated, saying, 'That man doesn't wear his gun on his hip like a farmer. Maybe we should let this one pass.'

"Wes was all puffed up after outdrawing a couple of guys in Barlow, and I remember that he called Clayton a chicken.

"Well, we rode up to the wagon. Wes said to the man, 'Old man, I really admire that Sharps you got in your scabbard. Think you should just hand it over to me.'

"Wes went for his gun. Then all hell broke loose. I swear, I never even saw that old guy reach for his gun. He was that fast. Suddenly, it was out and smokin', and Wes was on the ground, and Clayton was fallin' from his horse. I threw my hands in the air and hollered that I didn't want any part in it."

Darby narrowed his eyes suspiciously and said, "Describe this guy to me. Wes was fast as greased lightning. You say this guy was so fast you didn't even see him go for his gun?"

"Well ... like I said, he was an older guy ... maybe about your age ... maybe fifties. I don't know. I'm not good at guessin' age. He was dressed in buckskin, tall, thin, gray hair, gray mustache, and a real deep voice. The man was about to mount a grulla-colored horse when we rode up. You think you might know this guy?"

"Cleve, if that was who I think it was, you and Clayton are lucky to be alive. About five years ago, a pard and I drew down on a man fitting that description in a saloon. My pard was mighty fast with a gun too. He was killed, and I still carry the lead in my shoulder from that fight. About three years ago I saw that same man ride through Barlow, and I'm not ashamed to say I stayed clear of him. Seems like I remember his saddle was on a grulla-colored horse at the time."

"Who is he?"

"The man you just described could well be Truman Garrett."

Darby began to pack his saddlebags with his few belongings.

"Hey, you leaving?" asked Cleve with alarm in his voice. The older man was obviously packing. "What about Clayton here? He needs to rest."

"He's your pard. You take care of him. I'm riding north in the morning. I'll help you get Wes's body in the ground, and then I'm leaving. This country is getting too crowded for me. You and Clay would do best to ride out soon as he can travel."

"This guy really spooks you," observed Cleve with surprise.

"You want to cross him again?" questioned the older man.

"No! I'll stay clear of him."

"If this guy is traveling with a woman, it figures he's of a mind to settle down. Garrett's not only the fastest man with a gun I've ever seen. He's also an honest man. The way I see it, our way of rustling a calf or taking what we want from a farmer is over in this part of the country. It's time to move on or take up an honest trade. I'm too old to change. Don't know much about raising cattle and farming. You and Clayton are young enough to learn."

"Well, I figure we have enough meat left from that calf we rustled over at the Brewster homestead to last until Clayton's able to travel."

Clayton lay nearly motionless on his blankets. He appeared pale and barely conscious.

20

Light struggled to make it through the heavy clouds. Soon the outline of a wagon appeared and shadows turned into mules and horses as a little more silvery light filtered through the mist in the clearing. A small spark flickered into a flame under Truman's expert coaxing. Sallie rolled over inside the wagon and found the blanket beside her bare. She opened her eyes and slowly began to comprehend her surroundings. Seeing a dim gray light through the opening in the wagon canvas, she realized morning was dawning. Truman must be already up and preparing for what would surely be the last day of travel.

Quickly, she began to roll the blankets and put them into their place on the side of the wagon. Locating her shoes, she slipped her feet into them and laced them up. Thoughts of seeing the faces of her son and his wife and children caused her to smile as she reached for her hairbrush and toiletries. By the time she stepped down from the wagon, a fire was blazing in the misty morning air. Truman had a pot with some water boiling for coffee. That would be especially appreciated this morning due to the damp chill. With a little shiver, Sallie pulled her shawl tighter around her shoulders. Truman was kneeling to place another branch on the fire as she approached and bent to kiss his cheek. He smiled and returned the kiss.

"There are still some biscuits wrapped in a towel. Those will taste good with some of Marta's jam and hot coffee."

Sallie unwrapped the biscuits and opened the jam. Their simple breakfast was enjoyed beside the crackling fire. Soon the mist began to lift as morning advanced, promising a pleasant day ahead.

Fletcher's distinctive welcoming bray echoed in the quiet meadow as Truman walked out to gather the mules from their picket lines. The accented gasps of Fletcher's bray with little pauses in between always reminded Sallie of the sound of a rusty hinge on an opening gate. Truman soon had the mules hitched, and the wagon was ready to roll. He tied Sallie's horse and the grulla to the back of the wagon. The bay was chosen as his ride of the day. Sallie climbed onto the wagon seat, and, picking up the driving lines, was ready to go. Truman mounted the bay and took the lead as they began what they hoped would be the final day of travel. The frisky bay chomped at the bit as he flipped his head up and down, protesting the slow pace. He pranced, sidestepping along the road until he finally settled down.

The road gradually sloped downward, so the mules weren't working as hard as they were yesterday. They were stepping along at a brisk walk. It was almost as if they sensed the long journey was finally nearly over. Suddenly, through an opening in the trees, a little town came into view in the distance. The road curved again, and then the gently descending road led to the town's edge. It was now late morning and the little town was bustling with activity. Sallie realized this was the town her son, Jim, had described in one of his letters. There was Fuller's store, where he purchased supplies. His homestead was just on the other side of town. Oh, how she wished the team could hurry up. A feeling of excitement swept over her. She was really going to make it. There were times she had despaired of ever reaching this place. Sallie had so many stories to tell. What would Jim think of Truman? Truman seemed to sense her excitement. Turning in his saddle, he glanced back her way and smiled as their eyes met. The road leading away from town was winding but fairly level. Sallie carefully studied the landscape, searching for the landmarks Jim had described in his letter in order to find his place. Truman reined the bay to a halt and waited for the wagon to draw along side before continuing.

Sallie pointed to a particular outcropping of rock on a bluff overlooking the trail. "Jim said there would be a trail coming in from our right somewhere around here that we are to take."

Truman spotted the two wagon tracks first. "There it is."

They made the turn and continued on. Scattered trees blocked the view ahead. As they emerged from the trees, a homestead came into view. Sallie gasped and tears welled into her eyes as she realized this was the home her son had described.

Emotion choked her voice as she turned to Truman, riding beside her on the bay, and said, "There it is. It's just as Jim described it."

A young mother stepped out on the porch with a baby in her arms and a little boy following close behind. She had become aware of the sound of jingling harness, the creak of a wagon, and the rhythmic beat made by approaching hooves.

Movement along the road on top of the hill overlooking his property had also caught the attention of the young man approaching the porch where his wife stood. He shaded his eyes with his hand to better see a wagon pulled by a team of mules moving along the road.

"Who do you suppose it to be, Jim?"

"I can't tell for sure at this distance, but one of those horses tied at the back of the wagon is the same color as Mother's old horse, Joe."

The wagon slowed and then paused briefly at the entrance to the lane leading down to the young couple's cabin. As conviction took hold of the young man as to the identity of at least the female passenger on the wagon seat, he briskly walked to meet the wagon that was now beginning to make the turn into his lane.

Sallie could contain herself no longer. Halting the team and handing the driving lines to Truman, who sat astride his horse alongside the wagon seat, she climbed down from the wagon and hurried with arms outstretched to embrace her son.

"Jim, oh, Jim, we made it!"

"Mother!"

Jim's wife, Jenny, hugged her next with baby, Caroline, in her arms.

Sallie knelt, and shyly, little Charlie gave his grandma a hug.

"We told him you were coming. He watches the road every day," explained Jenny.

Truman had stepped down from his horse and was standing a little behind Sallie. Sallie turned, and, reaching for his hand, introduced him to her family.

"Jim, Jenny, I want you to meet Truman Garrett. We were married by Pastor Schaefer on the wagon train. Oh, there is so much to tell you. I would not have made it out here if it were not for Truman."

Little Charlie was obviously fascinated by Truman. As the adults chatted, and Jim proudly pointed out the work he had done to the homestead, Charlie was watching Truman and slowly edging closer.

Truman couldn't help but think how much Charlie reminded him of Jeremy. Squatting down to the little boy's level, he asked, "Hey, boy, what do you have there?" Truman was immediately rewarded with a grin as the little guy came forward to display the little wooden pony his dad had carved.

Jim motioned toward the little cabin, barn, and corral across the road from his place. "I figured you might like the Walkers' place. Jeb Walker decided to move back east after his wife died. I bought the cabin, barn, and forty acres. The house is small, but clean. The Walkers came in with the same group of settlers as Jenny and I. Jeb decided to take his little boy and go back east to be near family after his wife, Suzie, died."

While the mules waited patiently, the two families walked across the road to look at the Walkers' place. A porch went the whole length of the front of the cabin, just like Jim and Jenny's place. A few little flowers were blooming along the edge of the porch, and a vine wrapping itself around a corner support of the porch roof appeared to be a morning glory. Sallie felt as if the house was welcoming her home.

Upon opening the front door, they could see that the cabin was divided into two rooms. A wood stove and a table with chairs had been left behind in the main room. A curtain separated what must've been the bedroom from the main room. A little lean-to was in the back, where wood could be kept dry in the winter.

Truman and Sallie's eyes met. He nodded, and Sallie exclaimed, "This will be perfect!"

The baby started to fuss a little. Jenny said, "I'll get some dinner started."

"I'll give you a hand," offered Sallie, and she followed Jenny across the road. Jim and Jenny's cabin was slightly larger than the Walkers'. The main living area was more spacious with two small side rooms.

Truman and Jim walked back across the road to the wagon. Little Charlie had followed the men. When Truman asked Charlie if he'd like a ride in the wagon, the little guy nodded. So Truman lifted him onto the wagon seat. Truman and Jim, with Charlie seated in between, turned the team and drove the wagon into the front yard of the Walkers' cabin. The men soon had the mules unhitched and the horses situated in the little pasture beside the house. The animals were glad to be unhitched and commenced to roll. Soon they were contentedly grazing in the lush pasture.

The men then began to unload the wagon. Jim shared some of his dreams for his homestead's future. Truman found himself remembering what it was like starting out with his own place so many years ago. He realized Jim reminded him a little of himself back then. It wasn't long before they were called to dinner. The men continued in conversation as they crossed the road back to Jim's cabin. Truman was thinking with amazement that he was no longer a loner. He now had a wife and a family. He smiled. It had never crossed his mind that accepting the job offer from McMasters might change his life. Truman had found his heart again on the trail west.

They sat down to the homemade table, set with china brought all the way from Iowa. Jim prayed, asking a blessing for the food and thanking the

Lord for bringing his mother and Truman safely to their new home. After the prayer, Sallie looked around the room for a moment at her loved ones' faces, thinking, *I'm here. I'm really here—and with so much to be thankful for this day. My heart is truly full of joy. Just think, if I had not started on that trail, I would not have found Truman and not be here with Jim and his family.*

It was truly a trail of the heart.